YOU ARE IN THE MIND OF LUDWIG VAN BEETHOVEN as a modern music professor takes a trip back through time to the point where madness and genius meet and explode

YOU ARE IN COMMUNICATION WITH THE UNCANNY UNKNOWN as a pretty woman professor receives warnings of physical danger and sexual treachery from a mysterious and macabre message service

YOU ARE IN A BAR FILLED WITH GREMLINS AND OTHER HORRORS as a man on a mind-blowing binge uncorks a bottle of spirits more bubbly than champagne and more potent than any liquor ever distilled

YOU ARE IN THE HANDS OF EIGHT EXPERTS IN EXCITEMENT in a collection that crosses new boundaries and breaks through all barriers to bring you the best science fiction being created today

ABOUT THE EDITOR:
TERRY CARR is recognized as one of the major editors of modern science fiction. He has been awarded seven Nebula Citations by the Science Fiction Writers of America. Also well known as a science fiction writer, historian, and lecturer, he makes his home in California.

"There is a basic unity in the unique taste of Terry Carr which makes this book an entity as much as a collection." —*Galileo*

The UNIVERSE series, edited by Terry Carr, is available in Popular Library editions:

UNIVERSE 3
00234-4 $1.25

UNIVERSE 4
00290-5 $1.25

UNIVERSE 5
00353-7 $1.25

UNIVERSE 6
04034-3 $1.50

UNIVERSE 7

Edited by Terry Carr

POPULAR LIBRARY • NEW YORK

UNIVERSE 7

Published by Popular Library, a unit of CBS Publications, the Consumer Publishing Division of CBS Inc., by arrangement with Doubleday & Company, Inc.

ISBN: 0-445-04269-9

Printed in the United States of America

10 9 8 7 6 5 4 3 2 1

CONTENTS

Science fiction is difficult to define: every time someone offers a new definition, a dozen students of the genre come forth grinning to point out famous sf stories that would be excluded by it, or stories it **would** include which are obviously not science fiction. Even such a simple rule as "Science fiction stories must stem from extrapolations of currently accepted science" begs too many questions, for what are we to call stories written about a jungle-covered Venus before our knowledge of that planet made the setting clearly impossible, or of trips to the microcosm of the atom based on the theories of nineteenth-century scientists? Can a story be science fiction one year and change to fantasy the next without a word being altered?

Fritz Leiber, who has won awards for every kind of story from sword-and-sorcery (**Ill Met in Lankhmar**) to "pure" science fiction (**The Wanderer**), doesn't concern himself with definitions—except, perhaps, to flout them playfully. Here he offers a delightful novelette about a young genius in a top-secret research installation who explores the implications of a great scientist's theories. Authentic science fiction, you say? Even if the theories are those of Pythagoras?

A RITE OF SPRING

Fritz Leiber

This is the story of the knight in shining armor and the princess imprisoned in a high tower, only with the roles reversed. True, young Matthew Fortree's cell was a fabulously luxurious, quaintly furnished suite in the vast cube of the most secret Coexistence Complex in the American Southwest, not terribly far from the U. S. Government's earlier most secret project, the nuclear one. And he was free to roam most of the rest of the cube whenever he wished. But there were weightier reasons which really did make him the knight in shining armor imprisoned in the high tower: his suite was on the top, or mathematicians', floor and the cube was very tall and he rarely wished to leave his private quarters except for needful meals and exercise, medical appointments, and his unonerous specified duties; his unspecified duties were more taxing. And while he did not have literal shining armor, he did have some very handsome red silk pajamas delicately embroidered with gold.

With the pajamas he wore soft red leather Turkish slippers, the toes of which actually turned up, and a red nightcap with a tassel, while over them and around his spare, short frame he belted tightly a fleece-lined long black dressing gown of heavier, ribbed silk also embroidered with gold, somewhat more floridly. If Matthew's social daring had equaled his flamboyant tastes, he would in public have worn small clothes and a powdered wig and swung a court sword at his side,

8

for he was much enamored of the Age of Reason and yearned to quip wittily in a salon filled with appreciative young Frenchwomen in daringly low-cut gowns, or perhaps only one such girl. As it was, he regularly did wear gray kid gloves, but that was partly a notably unsuccessful effort to disguise his large powerful hands, which sorted oddly with his slight, almost girlish figure.

The crueler of Math's colleagues (he did not like to be called Matt) relished saying behind his back that he had constructed a most alluring love nest, but that the unknown love bird he hoped to trap never deigned to fly by. In this they hit the mark, as cruel people so often do, for young mathematicians need romantic sexual love, and pine away without it, every bit as much as young lyric poets, to whom they are closely related. In fact, on the night this story begins, Math had so wasted away emotionally and was gripped by such a suicidally extreme Byronic sense of futility and Gothic awareness of loneliness that he had to bite his teeth together harshly and desperately compress his lips to hold back sobs as he knelt against his mockingly wide bed with his shoulders and face pressed into its thick, downy, white coverlet, as if to shut out the mellow light streaming on him caressingly from the tall bedside lamps with pyramidal jet bases and fantastic shades built up of pentagons of almost paper-thin, translucent ivory joined with silver leading. This light was strangely augmented at irregular intervals.

For it was a Gothic night too, you see. A dry thunderstorm was terrorizing the desert outside with blinding flashes followed almost instantly by deafening crashes which reverberated very faintly in the outer rooms of the Complex despite the mighty walls and partitions, which were very thick, both to permit as nearly perfect soundproofing as possible (so the valuable ideas of the solitary occupants might mature with-

9

out disturbance, like mushrooms in a cave) and also to allow for very complicated, detection-proof bugging. In Math's bedroom, however, for a reason which will be made clear, the thunderclaps were almost as loud as outside, though he did not start at them or otherwise show he even heard them. They were, nevertheless, increasing his Gothic mood in a geometrical progression. While the lightning flashes soaked through the ceiling. a point also to be explained later. Between flashes, the ceiling and walls were very somber, almost black, yet glimmering with countless tiny random highlights like an indoor Milky Way or the restlessly shifting points of light our eyes see in absolute darkness. The thick-piled black carpet shimmered similarly.

Suddenly Matthew Fortree started up on his knees and bent his head abruptly back. His face was a grimacing mask of self-contempt as he realized the religious significance of his kneeling posture and the disgusting religiosity of what he was about to utter, for he was a devout atheist, but the forces working within him were stronger than shame.

"Great Mathematician, hear me!" he cried hoarsely aloud, secure in his privacy and clutching at Eddington's phrase to soften a little the impact on his conscience of his hateful heresy. "Return me to the realm of my early childhood, or otherwise moderate my torments and my loneliness, or else terminate this life I can no longer bear!"

As if in answer to his prayer there came a monstrous flash-and-crash dwarfing all of the storm that had gone before. The two lamps arced out, plunging the room into darkness through which swirled a weird jagged wildfire, as if all the electricity in the wall-buried circuits, augmented by that of the great flash, had escaped to lead a brief free life of its own, like ball lightning or St. Elmo's fire.

(This event was independently confirmed beyond question or doubt. As thousands in the big cube testified, all the lights in the Coexistence Complex went out for one minute and seventeen seconds. Many heard the crash, even in rooms three or four deep below the outermost layer. Several score saw the wildfire. Dozens felt tingling electric shocks. Thirteen were convinced at the time that they had been struck by lightning. Three persons died of heart failure at the instant of the big flash, as far as can be determined. There were several minor disasters in the areas of medical monitoring and continuous experiments. Although a searching investigation went on for months, and still continues on a smaller scale, no completely satisfactory explanation has ever been found, though an odd rumor continues to crop up that the final monster flash was induced by an ultrasecret electrical experiment which ran amuck, or else succeeded too well, all of which resulted in a permanent increment in the perpetual nervousness of the masters of the cube.)

The monster stroke was the last one of the dry storm. Two dozen or so seconds passed. Then against the jagged darkness and the ringing silence, Math heard his door's mechanical bell chime seven times. (He'd insisted on the bell being installed in such a way as to replace the tiny fish-eye lens customary on all the cube's cubicles. Surely the designer was from Manhattan!)

He struggled to his feet, half blinded, his vision still full of the wildfire (or afterimages) so like the stuff of ocular migraine. He partly groped, partly remembered his way out of the bedroom, shutting the door behind him, and across the living room to the outer door. He paused there to reassure himself that his red nightcap was set properly on his head, the tassel falling to the right, and his black robe securely belted. Then he took a deep breath and opened the door.

Like his suite, the corridor was steeped in darkness and aswirl with jaggedy, faint blues and yellows. Then, at the level of his eyes, he saw two brighter, twinkling points of green light about two and a half inches horizontally apart. A palm's length below them was another such floating emerald. At the height of his chest flashed another pair of the green points, horizontally separated by about nine inches. At waist level was a sixth, and a hand's length directly below that, a seventh. They moved a bit with the rest of the swirling, first a little to the left, then to the right, but maintained their positions relative to each other.

Without consciousness of having done any thinking, sought any answers, it occurred to him that they were what might be called the seven crucial points of a girl: eyes, chin, nipples, umbilicus, and the center of all wonder and mystery. He blinked his eyes hard, but the twinkling points were still there. The migraine spirals seemed to have faded a little, but the seven emeralds were bright as ever and still flashed the same message in their cryptic positional Morse. He even fancied he saw the shimmer of a clinging dress, the pale triangle of an elfin face in a flow of black hair, and pale serpents of slender arms.

Behind and before him the lights blazed on, and there, surely enough, stood a slim young woman in a long dark-green grandmother's skirt and a frilly salmon blouse, sleeveless but with ruffles going up her neck to her ears. Her left hand clutched a thick envelope purse sparkling with silver sequins, her right dragged a coat of silver fox. While between smooth black cascades and from under black bangs, an elfin face squinted worriedly into his own through silver-rimmed spectacles.

Her gaze stole swiftly and apologetically up and down him, without hint of a smile, let alone giggle, at either his nightcap and its tassel, or the turned-up toes of his Turkish slippers, and then returned to confront him anxiously.

He found himself bowing with bent left knee, right foot advanced, right arm curved across his waist, left arm trailing behind, eyes still on hers (which *were* green), and he heard himself say, "Matthew Fortree, at your service, mademoiselle."

Somehow, she seemed French. Perhaps because of the raciness of the emeralds' twinkling message, though only the top two of them had turned out to be real.

Her accent confirmed this when she answered, " 'Sank you. I am Severeign Saxon, sir, in search of my brother. And mooch scared. 'Scuse me."

Math felt a pang of delight. Here was a girl as girls should be, slim, soft-spoken, seeking protection, calling him sir, not moved to laughter by his picturesque wardrobe, and favoring the fond, formal phrases he liked to use when he talked to himself. The sort of girl who, interestingly half undressed, danced through his head on lonely nights abed.

That was what he felt. What he did, quite characteristically, was frown at her severely and say, "I don't recall any Saxon among the mathematicians, madam, although it's barely possible there is a new one I haven't met."

"Oh, but my brother has not my name . . ." she began hurriedly, then her eyelashes fluttered, she swayed and caught herself. *"Pardonne,"* she went on faintly, gasping a little. "Oh, do not think me forward, sir, but might I not come in and catch my breath? I am frightened by ze storm, I have searched so long, and ze halls are so lonely . . ."

Inwardly cursing his gauche severity, Math instantly

13

resumed his courtly persona and cried softly, "*Your* pardon, madam. Come in, come in by all means and rest as long as you desire." Shaping the beginning of another bow, he took her trailing coat and wafted her past him inside. His fingertips tingled at the incredibly smooth, cool, yet electric texture of her skin.

He hung up her coat, marveling that the silky fur was not so softly smooth as his fingertips' memory of her skin, and found her surveying his spacious sanctum with its myriad shelves and spindly little wallside tables.

"Oh, sir, this room is like fairyland," she said, turning to him with a smile of delight. "Tell me, are all zoze tiny elephants and ships and lacy spheres ivory?"

"They are, madam, such as are not jet," he replied quite curtly. He had been preparing a favorable, somewhat flowery, but altogether sincere comparison of her pale complexion to the hue of his ivories (and of her hair to his jets), but something, perhaps "fairyland," had upset him. "And now will you be seated, Miss Saxon, so you may rest?"

"Oh, yes, sir . . . Mr. Fortree," she replied flusteredly, and let herself be conducted to a long couch facing a TV screen set in the opposite wall. With a bob of her head she hurriedly seated herself. He had intended to sit beside her, or at least at the other end of the couch, but a sudden gust of timidity made him stride to the farthest chair, a straight-backed one, facing the couch, where he settled himself bolt upright.

"Refreshment? Some coffee perhaps?"

She gulped and nodded without lifting her eyes. He pushed a button on the remote control in the left-hand pocket of his dressing gown and felt more in command of the situation. He fixed his eyes on his guest and, to his horror, said harshly, "What is your number, madam . . . of years?" he finished in a voice less bold.

He had intended to comment on the storm and its abrupt end, or inquire about her brother's last name, or even belatedly compare her complexion to ivory and her skin to fox fur, anything but demand her age like some police interrogator. And even then not simply, "Say, would you mind telling me how old you are?" but to phrase it so stiltedly . . . Some months back, Math had gone through an acute attack of sesquipedalianism—of being unable to find the simple word for anything, or even a circumlocution, but only a long, usually Latin one. Attending his first formal reception in the Complex, he had coughed violently while eating a cookie. The hostess, a formidably poised older lady, had instantly made solicitous inquiry. He wanted to answer, "I got a crumb in my nose," but could think of nothing but "nasal cavity," and when he tried to say that, there was another and diabolic misfire in his speech centers, and what came out was, "I got a crumb in my navel."

The memory of it could still reduce him to jelly.

"Seven—" he heard her begin. Instantly his feelings did another flip-flop and he found himself thinking of how nice it would be, since he himself was only a few years into puberty, if she were younger still.

"Seventeen?" he asked eagerly.

And now it was her mood that underwent a sudden change. No longer downcast, her eyes gleamed straight at him, mischievously, and she said, "No, sir, I was about to copy your 'number of years' and say 'seven and a score.' And now I am of a mind not to answer your rude question at all." But she relented and went on with a winning smile, "No, seven and a decade, only seventeen—that's my age. But to tell the truth, sir, I thought you were asking my ruling number. And I answered you. Seven."

"Do you mean to tell me you believe in numerology?" Math demanded, his concerns doing a third instant flip-flop. Acrobatic moods are a curse of adolescence.

She shrugged prettily. "Well, sir, among the sciences—"

"Sciences, madam?" he thundered like a small Doctor Johnson. "Mathematics itself is not a science, but only a game men have invented and continue to play. The supreme game, no doubt, but still only a game. And that you should denominate as a science that . . . that farrago of puerile superstitions—! Sit still now, madam, and listen carefully while I set you straight."

She crouched a little, her eyes apprehensively on his.

"The first player of note of the game of mathematics," he launched out in lecture-hall tones, "was a Greek named Pythagoras. In fact, in a sense he probably invented the game. Yes, surely he did—twenty-five centuries ago, well before Archimedes, before Aristotle. But those were times when men's minds were still befuddled by the lies of the witch doctors and priests, and so Pythagoras (or his followers, more likely!) conceived the mystical notion"—his words dripped sarcastic contempt—"that numbers had a real existence of their own, as if—"

She interrupted rapidly. "But do they not? Like the little atoms we cannot see, but which—"

"Silence, Sovereign!"

"But Matthew—"

"Silence, I said!—as if numbers came from another realm or world, yet had power over this one—"

"That's what the little atoms have—power, especially when they explode." She spoke with breathless rapidity.

"—and as if numbers had all kinds of individual qualities, even personalities—some lucky, some unlucky, some good, some bad, et cetera—as if they

16

were real beings, even gods! I ask you, have you ever heard of anything more ridiculous than numbers— mere pieces in a game—being alive? Yes, of course— the idea of gods being real. But with the Pythagoreans (they became a sort of secret society) such nonsense was the rule. For instance, Pythagoras was the first man to analyze the musical scale mathematically—brilliant!—but then he (his followers!) went on to decide that some scales (the major) are stimulating and healthy and others (the minor) unhealthy and sad—"

Severeign interjected swiftly yet spontaneously. "Yes, I've noticed that, sir. Major keys make me feel 'appy, minor keys sad—no, pleasantly melancholy . . ."

"Autosuggestion! The superstitions of the Pythagoreans became endless—the transmigration of souls, metempsychosis (a psychosis, all right!), reincarnation, immortality, you name it. They even refused to eat beans—"

"They were wrong there. Beans cassolette—"

"Exactly! In the end, Plato picked up their ideas and carried them to still sillier lengths. Wanted to outlaw music in minor scales—like repealing the law of gravity! He also asserted that not only numbers, but all ideas were more real than things—"

"But excuse me, sir—I seem to recall hearing my brother talk about real numbers . . ."

"Sheer semantics, madam! Real numbers are merely the most primitive and obvious ones in the parlor game we call mathematics. Q.E.D."

And with that, he let out a deep breath and subsided, his arms folded across his chest.

She said, "You have quite overwhelmed me, sir. Henceforth I shall call seven only my favorite number . . . if I may do that?"

"Of course you may. God (excuse the word) forbid I ever try to dictate to you, madam."

With that, silence descended, but before it could become uncomfortable, Math's remote control purred discreetly in his pocket and prodded him in the thigh. He busied himself fetching the coffee on a silver tray in hemispheres of white eggshell china, whose purity of form Sovereign duly admired.

They made a charming couple together, looking surprisingly alike, quite like brother and sister, the chief differences being his more prominent forehead, large strong hands, and forearms a little thick with the muscles that powered the deft fingers. All of which made him seem like a prototype of man among the animals, a slight and feeble being except for hands and brain—manipulation and thought.

He took his coffee to his distant chair. The silence returned and did become uncomfortable. But he remained tongue-tied, lost in bitter reflections. Here the girl of his dreams (why not admit it?) had turned up, and instead of charming her with courtesies and witticisms, he had merely become to a double degree his unpleasant, critical, didactic, quarrelsome, rejecting, lonely self, perversely shrinking from all chances of warm contact. Better find out her brother's last name and send her on her way. Still, he made a last effort.

"How may I entertain you, madam?" he asked lugubriously.

"Any way you wish, sir," she answered meekly.

Which made it worse, for his mind instantly became an unbearable blank. He concentrated hopelessly on the toes of his red slippers.

"There *is* something we could do," he heard her say tentatively. "We could play a game . . . if you'd care to. Not chess or go or any sort of mathematical game—there I couldn't possibly give you enough competition—but something more suited to my scatter brain, yet which would, I trust, have enough complications to amuse you. The Word Game . . ."

Once more Math was filled with wild delight, unconscious of the wear and tear inflicted on his system by these instantaneous swoops and soarings of mood. This incredibly perfect girl had just proposed they do the thing he loved to do more than anything else, and at which he invariably showed at his dazzling best. Play a game, any game!

"Word Game?" he asked cautiously, almost suspiciously. "What's that?"

"It's terribly simple. You pick a category, say Musicians with names beginning with B, and then you—"

"Bach, Beethoven, Brahms, Berlioz, Bartok, C. P. E. Bach (J.S.' son)," he rattled off.

"Exactly! Oh, I can see you'll be much too good for me. When we play, however, you can only give one answer at one time and then wait for me to give another—else you'd win before I ever got started."

"Not at all, madam. I'm mostly weak on words," he assured her, lying in his teeth.

She smiled and continued, "And when one player can't give another word or name in a reasonable time, the other wins. And now, since I suggested the Game, I insist that in honor of you, and my brother, but without making it at all mathematical really, we play a subvariety called the Numbers Game."

"Numbers Game?"

She explained, "We pick a small cardinal number, say between one and twelve, inclusive, and alternately name groups of persons or things traditionally associated with it. Suppose we picked four (we won't); then the right answers would be things like the Four Gospels, or the Four Horsemen of the Apocalypse—"

"Or of Notre Dame. How about units of time and vectors? Do they count as things?"

She nodded. "The four seasons, the four major points of the compass. Yes. And now, sir, what number shall we choose?"

He smiled fondly at her. She really was lovely—a jewel, a jewel green as her eyes. He said like a courtier, "What other, madam, than your favorite?"

"Seven. So be it. Lead off, sir."

"Very well." He had been going to insist politely that she take first turn, but already gamesmanship was vying with courtesy, and the first rule of gamesmanship is, Snatch Any Advantage You Can.

He started briskly, "The seven crucial—" and instantly stopped, clamping his lips.

"Go on, sir," she prompted. " 'Crucial' sounds interesting. You've got me guessing."

He pressed his lips still more tightly together, and blushed—at any rate, he felt his cheeks grow hot. Damn his treacherous, navel-fixated subconscious mind! Somehow it had at the last moment darted to the emerald gleams he'd fancied seeing in the hall, and he'd been within a hairsbreadth of uttering, "The seven crucial points of a girl."

"Yes . . . ?" she encouraged.

Very gingerly he parted his lips and said, his voice involuntarily going low, "The Seven Deadly Sins: Pride, Covetousness—"

"My, that's a stern beginning," she interjected. "I wonder what the crucial sins are?"

"—Envy, Sloth," he continued remorselessly.

"Those are the cold ones," she announced. "Now for the hot."

"Anger—" he began, and only then realized where he was going to end—and cursed the show-off impulse that had made him start to enumerate them. He forced himself to say, "Gluttony, and—" He shied then and was disastrously overtaken for the first time in months

20

by his old stammer. "Lul-lul-lul-lul-lul—" he trilled like some idiot bird.

"Lust," she cooed, making the word into another sort of bird call, delicately throaty. Then she said, "The seven days of the week."

Math's mind again became a blank, through which he hurled himself like a mad rat against one featureless white wall after another, until at last he saw a single dingy star. He stammered out, "The Seven Sisters, meaning the seven anti-trust laws enacted in 1913 by New Jersey while Woodrow Wilson was Governor."

"You begin, sir," she said with a delighted chuckle, "by scraping the bottom of your barrel, a remarkable feat. But I suppose that being a mathematician you get at the bottom of the barrel while it's still full by way of the fourth dimension."

"The fourth dimension is no hocus-pocus, madam, but only time," he reproved, irked by her wit and by her having helped him out when he first stuttered. "Your seven?"

"Oh. I could repeat yours, giving another meaning, but why not the Seven Seas?"

Instantly he saw a fantastic ship with a great eye at the bow sailing on them. "The seven voyages of Sinbad."

"The Seven Hills of Rome."

"The seven colors of the spectrum," he said at once, beginning to feel less fearful of going word-blind. "Though I can't imagine why Newton saw indigo and blue as different prismatic colors. Perhaps he wanted them to come out seven for some mystical reason—he had his Pythagorean weaknesses."

"The seven tones of the scale, as discovered by Pythagoras," she answered sweetly.

"Seven-card stud," he said, somewhat gruffly.

"Seven-up, very popular before poker."

21

"This one will give you one automatically," he said stingily. "However, a seventh son."

"And I'm to say the seventh son of a seventh son? But I cannot accept yours, sir. I said cardinal, not ordinal numbers. No sevenths, sir, if you please."

"I'll rephrase it then. Of seven sons, the last."

"Not allowed. I fear you quibble, sir." Her eyes widened, as if at her own temerity.

"Oh, very well. The Seven Against Thebes."

"The Epigoni, their sons."

"I didn't know there were seven of *them*," he objected.

"But there should be seven, for the sake of symmetry," she said wistfully.

"Allowed," he said, proud of his superior generosity in the face of a feminine whim. "The Seven Bishops."

"Dear Sancroft, Ken, and Company," she murmured. "The Seven Dials. In London. Does that make you think of time travel?"

"No, big newspaper offices. *The Seven Keys to Baldpate,* a book."

"*The Seven Samurai*, a Kurosawa film."

"*The Seventh Seal*, a Bergman film!" He was really snapping them out now, but—

"Oh, oh. No sevenths—remember, sir?"

"A silly rule—I should have objected at the start. The seven liberal arts, being the quadrivium (arithmetic, music, geometry, and astronomy) added to the trivium (grammar, logic, and rhetoric)."

"Delightful," she said. "The seven planets—"

"No, madam! There are nine."

"I was about to say," she ventured in a small, defenseless voice, "—of the ancients. The ones out to Saturn and then the sun and moon."

"Back to Pythagoras again!" he said with a quite un-

22

reasonable nastiness, glaring over her head. "Besides, that would make eight planets."

"The ancients didn't count the Earth as one." Her voice was even tinier.

He burst out with, "Earth not a planet, fourth dimension, time travel, indigo not blue, no ordinals allowed, the ancients—madam, your mind is a sink of superstitions!" When she did not deny it, he went on, "And now I'll give you the master answer: all groups of persons or things belong to the class of the largest successive prime among the odd numbers—your seven, madam!"

She did not speak. He heard a sound like a mouse with a bad cold, and looking at her, saw that she was dabbing a tiny handkerchief at her nose and cheeks. "I don't think I want to play the Game any more," she said indistinctly. "You're making it too mathematical."

How like a woman, he thought, banging his hand against his thigh. He felt the remote control and, on a savage impulse, jabbed another button. The TV came on. "Perhaps your mind needs a rest," he said unsympathetically. "See, we open the imbecile valve."

The TV channel was occupied by one of those murderous chases in a detective series (subvariety: military police procedural) where the automobiles became the real protagonists, dark passionate monsters with wills of their own to pursue and flee, or perhaps turn on their pursuer, while the drivers become grimacing puppets whose hands are dragged around by the steering wheels.

Math didn't know if his guest was watching the screen, and he told himself he didn't care—to suppress the bitter realization that instead of cultivating the lovely girl chance had tossed his way, he was browbeating her.

Then the chase entered a multistory garage, and he was lost in a topology problem on the order of: "Given

23

three entrances, two exits, n two-way ramps, and so many stories, what is the longest journey a car can make without crossing its path?" When Math had been a small child—even before he had learned to speak—his consciousness had for long periods been solely a limitless field, or even volume filled with points of light, which he could endlessly count and manipulate. Rather like the random patterns we see in darkness, only he could marshal them endlessly in all sorts of fascinating arrays, and wink them into or out of existence at will. Later he learned that at such times he had gone into a sort of baby-trance, so long and deep that his parents had become worried and consulted psychologists. But then words had begun to replace fields and sets of points in his mind, his baby-trances had become infrequent and finally vanished altogether, so that he was no longer able to enter the mental realm where he was in direct contact with the stuff of mathematics. Thinking about topological problems, such as that of the multilevel garage, was the closest he could get to it now. He had come from that realm "trailing clouds of glory," but with the years they had faded. Yet it was there, he sometimes believed, that he had done all his really creative work in mathematics, the work that had enabled him to invent a new algebra at the age of eleven. And it was there he had earlier tonight prayed the Great Mathematician to return him when he had been in a mood of black despair—which, he realized with mild surprise, he could no longer clearly recall, at least in its intensity.

He had solved his garage problem and was setting up another when, "License plates, license plates!" he heard Severeign cry out in the tones of one who shouts, "Onionsauce, onionsauce!" at baffled rabbits.

Her elfin face, which Math had assumed to be still tearful, was radiant.

24

"What about license plates?" he asked gruffly.

She jabbed a finger at the TV, where in the solemn finale of the detective show, the camera had just cut to the hero's thoroughly wrecked vehicle while he looked on from under bandages, and while the sound track gave out with taps. "Cars have them!"

"Yes, I know, but where does that lead?"

"Almost all of them have seven digits!" she announced triumphantly. "So do phone numbers!"

"You mean, you want to go on with the Game?" Math asked with an eagerness that startled him.

Part of her radiance faded. "I don't know. The Game is really dreadful. Once started, you can't get your mind off it until you perish of exhaustion of ideas."

"But you want nevertheless to continue?"

"I'm afraid we must. Sorry I got the megrims back there. And now I've gone and wasted an answer by giving two together. The second counts for yours. Oh well, my fault."

"Not at all, madam. I will balance it out by giving two at once too. The seven fat years and the seven lean years."

"Anyone would have got the second of those once you gave the first," she observed, saucily rabbiting her nose at him. "The number of deacons chosen by the Apostles in Acts. Nicanor's my favorite. Dear Nicky," she sighed, fluttering her eyelashes.

"Empson's Seven Types of Ambiguity," Math proclaimed.

"You're not enumerating?"

He shook his head. "Might get too ambiguous."

She flashed him a smile. Then her face slowly grew blank—with thought, he thought at first, but then with eyes half closed she murmured, "Sleepy."

25

"You want to rest?" he asked. Then, daringly, "Why not stretch out?"

She did not seem to hear. Her head drooped down. "Dopey too," she said somewhat indistinctly.

"Should I step up the air conditioning?" he asked. A wild fear struck him. "I assure you, madam, I didn't put anything in your coffee."

"And Grumpy!" she said triumphantly, sitting up. "Snow White's seven dwarfs!"

He laughed and answered, "The Seven Hunters, which are the Flannan Islands in the Hebrides."

"The Seven Sisters, a hybrid climbing rose, related to the rambler," she said.

"The seven common spectral types of stars—B-A-F-G-K-M . . . and O," he added a touch guiltily because O wasn't really a common type, and he'd never heard of this particular Seven (or Six, for that matter). She gave him a calculating look. Must be something else she's thinking of, he assured himself. Women don't know much astronomy except maybe the ancient sort, rubbed off from astrology.

She said, "The seven rays of the spectrum: radio, high frequency, infrared, visible, ultraviolet, X, and gamma." And she looked at him so bright-eyed that he decided she'd begun to fake a little too.

"And cosmic?" he asked sweetly.

"I thought those were particles," she said innocently.

He grumphed, wishing he could take another whack at the Pythagoreans. An equally satisfying target occurred to him—and a perfectly legitimate one, so long as you realized that this was a game that could be played creatively. "The Seven Subjects of Sensational Journalism: crime, scandal, speculative science, insanity, superstitions such as numerology, monsters, and millionaires."

Fixing him with a penetrating gaze, she immediately

intoned, "The Seven Sorrows of Shackleton: the crushing of the *Endurance* in the ice, the inhospitality of Elephant Island, the failure of the whaler *Southern Sky*, the failure of the Uruguayan trawler *Instituto de Pesca No. 1*, the failure on first use of the Chilean steamer *Yelcho*, the failure of the *Emma*, and the South Pole unattained!"

She continued to stare at him judicially. He realized he was starting to blush. He dropped his eyes and laughed uncomfortably. She chortled happily. He looked back at her and laughed with her. It was a very nice moment, really. He had cheated inventively and she had cheated right back at him the same way, pulling him up short without a word.

Feeling very, very good, very free, Math said, "The Seven Years War."

"The Seven Weeks War, between Prussia and Austria."

"The Seven Days War, between Israel and the Arabs."

"Surely Six?"

He grinned. "Seven. For six days the Israelis labored, and on the seventh day they rested."

She laughed delightedly, whereupon Math guffawed too.

She said, "You're witty, sir—though I can't allow that answer. I must tell my brother that one of his colleagues—" She stopped, glanced at her wrist, shot up. "I didn't realize it was so late. He'll be worried. Thanks for everything, Matthew—I've got to split." She hurried toward the door.

He got up too. "I'll get dressed and take you to his room. You don't know where it is. I'll have to find out."

She was reaching down her coat. "No time for that. And now I remember where."

27

He caught up with her as she was slipping her coat on. "But Sovereign, visitors aren't allowed to move around the Complex unescorted—"

"Oh pish!"

It was like trying to detain a busy breeze. He said desperately, "I won't bother to change."

She paused, grinned at him with uplifted brows, as though surprised and pleased. Then, "No, Matthew," settling her coat around her and opening the door.

He conquered his inhibitions and grabbed her by her silky shoulders—gently at the last moment. He faced her to him. They were exactly the same height.

"Hey," he asked smiling, "what about the Game?"

"Oh, we'll *have* to finish that. Tomorrow night, same time? G'bye now."

He didn't release her. It made him tremble. He started to say, "But Miss Saxon, you really can't go by yourself. After midnight all sorts of invisible eyes pick up anyone in the corridors."

He got as far as the "can't," when with a very swift movement she planted her lips precisely on his.

He froze, as if they had been paralysis darts—and he did feel an electric tingling. Even his invariable impulse to flinch was overridden, perhaps by the audacity of the contact. A self he'd never met said from a corner of his mind in the voice of Rex Harrison, "They're Anglo body-contact taboos, but not Saxon."

And then, between his parted lips and hers still planted on them, he felt an impossible third swift touch. There was a blind time—he didn't know how long—in which the universe filled with unimagined shocking possibility: tiny ondines sent anywhere by matter transmission, a live velvet ribbon from the fourth dimension, pet miniwatersnakes, a little finger with a strange silver ring on it poking out of a young witch's mouth . . . and then another sort of shocked

28

wonder, as he realized it could only have been her tongue.

His lips, still open, were pressing empty air. He looked both ways down the corridor. It was empty too. He quietly closed the door and turned to his ivory-lined room. He closed his lips and worked them together curiously. They still tingled, and so did a spot on his tongue. He felt very calm, not at all worried about Severeign being spotted, or who her brother was, or whether she would really come back tomorrow night. Although he almost didn't see the forest for the trees, it occurred to him that he was happy.

Next morning he felt the same, but very eager to tell someone all about it. This presented a problem, for Math had no friends among his colleagues. Yet a problem easily solved, after a fashion. Right after breakfast he hunted up Elmo Hooper.

Elmo was classed and quartered with the mathematicians, though he couldn't have told you the difference between a root and a power. He was an idiot savant, able to do lightning calculations and possessing a perfect eidetic memory. He was occasionally teamed with a computer to supplement its powers, and it was understood, as it is understood that some people will die of cancer, that he would eventually be permanently cyborged to one. In his spare time, of which he had a vast amount, he mooned around the Complex, ignored except when he came silently up behind gossipers and gave them fits because of his remarkable physical resemblance to Warren Dean, Coexistence's security chief. Both looked like young Vermont storekeepers and were equally laconic, though for different reasons.

Math, who though no lightning calculator, had a nearly eidetic memory himself, found Elmo the perfect confidant. He could tell him all his most private thoughts and feelings, and retrieve any of his previous remarks, knowing that Elmo would never retrieve any of them on his own initiative and never, never make a critical comment.

This morning he found Elmo down one floor in Physics, and soon was pouring out in a happy daze every detail about last night's visit and lovely visitor and all his amazing reactions to her, with no more thought for Elmo than he would have had for a combined dictaphone and information-storage-and-retrieval unit.

He would have been considerably less at ease had he known that Warren Dean regularly drained Elmo of all conversations by "sensitive" persons he overheard in his moonings. Though Math wouldn't have had to feel that way, for the dour security man had long since written Math off as of absolutely no interest to security, being anything but "sensitive" and quite incapable of suspicious contacts, or any other sort. (How else could you class a man who talked of nothing but ivories, hurt vanities, and pure abstractions?) If Elmo began to parrot Math, Dean would simply turn off the human bug, while what the bugs in Math's walls heard was no longer even taped.

Math's happy session with Elmo lasted until lunchtime, and he approached the Mathematics, Astronomy and Theoretical Physics Commons with lively interest. Telling the human memory bank every last thing he knew about Severeign had naturally transferred his attention to the things he didn't know about her, including the identity of her brother. He was still completely trustful that she would return at evening and answer his questions, but it would be nice to know a few things in advance.

The Commons was as gorgeous as Math's apartment, though less eccentrically so. It still gave him a pleasant thrill to think of all the pure intellect gathered here, busily chomping and chatting, though the presence of astronomers and especially theoretical physicists from the floor below added a sour note. Ah well, they weren't quite as bad as their metallurgical, hardware-mongering brothers. (These in turn were disgusted at having to eat with the chemists from the second floor below. The Complex, dedicated to nourishing all pure science, since that provably paid off better peacewise or warwise than applied science, arranged all the sciences by floors according to degree of purity and treated them according to the same standards, with the inhabitants of the top floor positively coddled. Actually, the Complex was devoted to the corruption of pure science, and realized that mathematics was at least fully as apt as any other discipline to turn up useful ideas. Who knew when a new geometry would not lead to a pattern of nuclear bombardment with less underkill? Or a novel topological concept point the way to the more efficient placement of offshore oil wells?)

So as Math industriously nibbled his new potatoes, fresh green peas, and roast lamb (the last a particularly tender mutation from the genetics and biology floors, which incidentally was a superb carrier of a certain newly developed sheep-vectored disease of the human nervous system), he studied the faces around him for ones bearing a resemblance to Severeign's—a pleasantly titillating occupation merely for its own sake. Although Math's colleagues believed the opposite, he was a sensitive student of the behavior of crowds, as any uninvolved spectator is apt to be. He had already noted that there was more and livelier conversation than usual and had determined that the increase was due to talk about last night's storm and power failure, with the physicists contributing rather more than their share, both about the storm and power failure and also about some other, though related topic which he hadn't yet identified.

31

While coffee was being served, Math decided on an unprecedented move: to get up and drift casually about in order to take a closer look at his candidates for Severeign's brother (or half brother, which would account elegantly for their different last names). And as invariably happens when an uninvolved spectator abandons that role and mixes in, it was at once noticed. Thinking of himself as subtly invisible as he moved about dropping nods and words here and there, he actually became a small center of attention. Whatever was that social misfit up to? (A harsh term, especially coming from members of a group with a high percentage of social misfits.) And why had he taken off his gray kid gloves? (In his new freedom he had simply forgotten to put them on.)

He saved his prime suspect until last, a wisp of a young authority on synthetic projective geometry named Angelo Spirelli, the spiral angel, whose floating hair was very black and whose face could certainly be described as girlish, though his eyes (Math noted on closer approach) were yellowish-brown, not green.

Unlike the majority, Spirelli was a rather careless, outgoing soul of somewhat racier and more voluble speech than his dreamy appearance might have led one to expect. "Hi, Fortree. Take a pew. What strange and unusual circumstance must I thank for this unexpected though pleasant encounter? The little vaudeville act Zeus and Hephaestus put on last night? One of the downstairs boys suspects collusion by the Complex."

Emboldened, Math launched into a carefully rehearsed statement. "At the big do last week I met a female who said she was related to you. A Miss Severeign Saxon."

Spirelli scowled at him, then his eyes enlarged happily. "Saxon, you say? Was she a squirmy little sexpot?"

32

Math's eyebrows lifted. "I suppose someone might describe her in that fashion." He didn't look as if he'd care much for such a someone.

"And you say you met her in El 'Bouk?"

"No, here at the fortnightly reception."

"That," Spirelli pronounced, scowling again, "does not add up."

"Well," Math said after a hiatus, "does it add down?"

Spirelli eyed him speculatively, then shrugged his shoulders with a little laugh. Leaning closer, he said, "Couple weeks ago I was into Albuquerque on a pass. At the Spurs 'n' Chaps this restless little saucer makes up to me. Says call her Saxon, don't know if it was supposed to be last name, first, or nick."

"Did she suggest you play a game?"

Spirelli grinned. "Games. I think so, but I never got around to finding out for sure. You see, she began asking me too many questions, like she was pumping me, and I remembered what Grandmother Dean teaches us at Sunday school about strange women, and I cooled her fast, feeling like a stupid, miserably well-behaved little choirboy. But a minute later Warren himself wanders in and I'm glad I did." His eyes swung, his voice dropped. "Speak of the devil."

Math looked. Across the Commons, Elmo Hooper—no, Warren Dean—had come in. Conversation did not die, but it did become muted—in waves going out from that point.

Math asked, "Did this girl in 'Bouk have black hair?"

Grown suddenly constrained, Spirelli hesitated, then said, "No, blond as they come. Saxon was a Saxon type."

After reaching this odd dead end, Math spent the rest of the afternoon trying to cool his own feelings about Sovereign, simply because they were getting too great. He was successful except that in the mathematics library *Webster's Unabridged*, second edition, tempted him to look up the "seven" entries (there were three columns), and he was halfway through them before he realized what he was doing. He finished them and resolutely shut the big book and his mind. He didn't think of Sovereign again until he finished dressing for bed, something he regularly did on returning to his room from dinner. It was a practice begun as a child to ensure he did nothing but study at night, but continued, with embellishments, when he began to think of himself as a gay young bachelor. He furiously debated changing back until he became irked at his agitation and decided to retain his "uniform of the night."

But he could no longer shut his mind on Sovereign. Here he was having an assignation (a word which simultaneously delighted him and gave him cold shivers) with a young female who had conferred on him a singular favor (another word that worked both ways, while the spot on his tongue tingled reminiscently). How should he behave? How would she behave? What would she expect of him? How would she react to his costume? (He redebated changing back.) Would she even come? Did he really remember what she looked like?

In desperation he began to look up everything on seven he could, including Shakespeare and ending with the Bible. A cross-reference had led him to the Book of Revelations, which he found surprisingly rich in that digit. He was reading, "And when he had opened the seventh seal, there was silence in heaven about the space of half an hour . . ." when, once again, there came the seven chimes at his door. He was there in a rush and had it open, and there was Sovereign, looking exactly like he remembered her—the three points of merry green eyes and tapered chin of flustered, trian-

34

gular elf-face, silver spectacles, salmon blouse and green grandmother's skirt (with line of coral buttons going down the one, and jade ones down the other), the sense of the other four crucial points of a girl under them, slender bare arms, one clutching silver-sequined purse, the other trailing coat of silver fox—and their faces as close together again as if the electric kiss had just this instant ended.

He leaned closer still, his lips parted, and he said, "The seven metals of the ancients: iron, lead, mercury, tin, copper, silver, and gold."

She looked as startled as he felt. Then a fiendish glint came into her eyes and she said, "The seven voices of the classical Greek actor: king, queen, tyrant, hero, old man, young man, maiden—that's me."

He said, "The Island of the Seven Cities. Antilia, west of Atlantis."

She said, "The seven Portuguese bishops who escaped to that island."

He said, "The Seven Caves of Aztec legend."

She said, "The Seven Walls of Ekbatana in old Persia: white, black, scarlet, blue, orange, silver and (innermost) golden."

He said, " 'Seven come Eleven,' a folk cry."

She said, "The Seven Cities of Cibola. All golden."

"But which turned out to be merely the pueblos of the Zuni," he jeered.

"Do you always have to deprecate?" she demanded. "Last night the ancients, the Pythagoreans. Now some poor aborigines."

He grinned. "Since we're on Amerinds, the Seven Council Fires, meaning the Sioux, Tetons, and so forth."

She scowled at him and said, "The Seven Tribes of the Tetons, such as the Hunkpapa."

Math said darkly, "I think you studied up on seven
35

and then conned me into picking it. *Seven Came Through*, a book by Eddie Rickenbacker."

"The Seven Champions of Christendom. Up Saint Dennis of France! To the death! No, I didn't, but you know, I sometimes feel I know everything about sevens, past, present, or future. It's strange."

They had somehow got to the couch and were sitting a little apart but facing each other, totally engrossed in the Game.

"Hmph! Up Saint David of Wales!" he said. "The Seven Churches in Asia Minor addressed in Revelations. Thyatira, *undsoweiter*."

"Philadelphia, too. The seven golden candlesticks, signifying the Seven Churches. Smyrna's really my favorite—I like figs." She clenched her fist with the tip of her thumb sticking out between index and middle fingers. Math wondered uncomfortably if she knew the sexual symbolism of the gesture. She asked, "Why are you blushing?"

"I'm not. The Seven Stars, meaning the Seven Angels of the Seven Churches."

"You were! And it got you so flustered you've given me one. The Seven Angels!"

"I'm not any more," he continued unperturbed, secure in his knowledge that he'd just read part of Revelations. "The seven trumpets blown by the Seven Angels."

"The beast with seven heads, also from Revelations. He also had the mouth of a lion and the feet of a bear *and* ten horns, but he looked like a leopard."

"The seven consulships of Gaius Marius," he said.

"The seven eyes of the Lamb," she countered.

"The Seven Spirits of God, another name for the Seven Angels, I think."

"All right. The seven sacraments."

"Does that include exorcism?" he wanted to know.

36

"No, but it does include order, which ought to please your mathematical mind."

"Thanks. The Seven Gifts of the Holy Ghost. Say, I know tongues, prophecy, vision, and dreams, but what are the other three?"

"Those are from Acts two—an interesting notion. But try Isaiah eleven—wisdom, understanding, counsel, might, knowledge, fear of the Lord, and righteousness."

Math said, "Whew, that's quite a load."

"Yes. On with the Game! To the death! The seven steps going up to Ezekiel's gate. Zeek forty twenty-six."

"Let's change religions," he said, beginning to feel snowed under by Christendom and the Bible. "The seven Japanese gods of luck."

"Or happiness. The seven major gods of Hinduism: Brahma, Vishnu, Siva, Varuna, Indra, Agni, and Surya. Rank male chauvinism! They didn't even include Lakshmi, the goddess of luck."

Math said sweetly, "The Seven Mothers, meaning the seven wives of the Hindu gods."

"Chauvinism, I said! Wives indeed! *Seven Daughters of the Theater*, a book by Edward Wagenknecht."

"The seven ages of man," Math announced, assuming a Shakespearean attitude. "At first the infant, mewling and puking—"

"And then the whining schoolboy—"

"And then the lover," he cut in, in turn, "sighing like furnace, with a woeful ballad made to his mistress' eyebrow."

"Have you ever sighed like furnace, Matthew?"

"No, but . . ." And raising a finger for silence, he scowled in thought.

"What are you staring at?" she asked.

"Your left eyebrow. Now listen . . .

37

Slimmest crescent of delight,
Why set so dark in sky so light?
My mistress' brow is whitest far;
Her eyebrow—the black evening star!"

"But it's not woeful," she objected. "Besides, how can the moon be a star?"

"As easily as it can be a planet—your ancients, madam. In any case, I invoke poetic license."

"But my eyebrow bends the wrong way for setting," she persisted. "Its ends point at the earth instead of skyward."

"Not if you were standing on your head, madam," he countered.

"But then my skirt would set too, showing my stockings. Shocking. Sir, I refuse! The Seven Sisters, meaning the Pleiades, those little stars."

Matthew's eyes lit up. He grinned excitedly. "Before I give you my next seven I want to show you yours," he told her, standing up.

"What do you mean?"

"I'll show you. Follow me," he said mysteriously and led her into his bedroom.

While she was ooh-ahing at the strangely glimmering black floor, walls, and ceiling, the huge white-fleeced bed, the scattered ivories which included the five regular solids of Pythagoras, the jet bedside lamps with their shades that were dodecahedrons of silver-joined pentagons of translucent ivory—and all the other outward signs of the U. S. Government's coddling of Matthew—he moved toward the lamps and switched them off, so the only light was that which had followed them into the bedroom.

Then he touched another switch and with the faintest whir and rustling the ceiling slowly parted like the Red Sea and moved aside, showing the desert night crusted with stars. The Coexistence Complex really catered to their mathematicians, and when Matthew had somewhat diffidently (for him) mentioned his fancy, they had seen no difficulty in removing the entire ceiling of his bedroom and the section of flat roof above and replacing them with a slightly domed plate-glass skylight, and masking it below with an opaque fabric matching the walls, which would move out of the way sidewise and gather in little folds at the urging of an electric motor.

Severeign caught her breath.

"Stars of the winter sky," Matthew said with a sweep of his arm and then began to point. "Orion. Taurus the bull with his red-eye Aldeberan. And, almost overhead, your Pleiades, madam. While there to the north is my reply. The Big Dipper, madam, also called the Seven Sisters."

Their faces were pale in the splendid starlight and the glow seeping from the room they'd left. They were standing close. Severeign did not speak at once. Instead she lifted her hand, forefinger and middle finger spread and extended, slowly toward his eyes. He involuntarily closed them. He heard her say, "The seven senses. Sight. And hearing." He felt the side of her hand lightly brush his neck. "Touch. No, keep your eyes closed." She laid the back of her hand against his lips. He inhaled with a little gasp. "Smell," came her voice. "That's myrrh, sir." His lips surprised him by opening and kissing her wrist. "And now you've added taste too, sir. Myrrh is bitter." It was true.

"But that's all the senses," he managed to say, "and you said seven. In common usage there are only five."

"Yes, that's what Aristotle said," she answered dryly. She pressed her warm palm against the curve of his jaw. "But there's heat too." He grasped her wrist and brought it down. She pulled her hand to free it and he automatically gripped it more tightly for a moment before letting go.

"And kinesthesia," she said. "You felt it in your muscles then. That makes seven."

He opened his eyes. Her face was close to his. He said, "Seventh heaven. No, that's an ordinal—"

"It will do, sir," she said. She knelt at his feet and looked up. In the desert starlight her face was solemn as a child's. "For my next seven I must remove your handsome Turkish slippers," she apologized.

He nodded, feeling lost in a dream, and lifted first one foot, then the other, as she did it.

As she rose, her hands went to his gold-worked black dressing gown. "And this too, sir," she said softly. "Close your eyes once more."

He obeyed, feeling still more dream-lost. He heard the slithering hrush of his robe dropping to the floor, he felt the buttons of his handsome red silk pajama tops loosened one by one from the top down, as her little fingers worked busily, and then the drawstring of the bottoms loosened.

He felt his ears lightly touched in their centers. She breathed, "The seven natural orifices of the male body, sir." The fingers touched his nostrils, brushed his mouth. "That's five, sir." Next he was briefly touched where only he had ever touched himself before. There was an electric tingling, like last night's kiss. The universe seemed to poise around him. Finally he was touched just as briefly where he'd only been touched by his doctor. His universe grew.

He opened his eyes. Her face was still child-grave. The light shining past him from the front room was enough to show the green of her skirt, the salmon of her blouse, the ivory of her skin dancing with starlight. He felt electricity running all over his body. He swallowed with difficulty, then said harshly, "For my next seven, madam, you must undress."

There was a pause. Then, "Myself?" she asked. "*You* didn't have to." She closed her eyes and blushed, first delicately under her eyes, along her cheekbones, then richly over her whole face, down to the salmon ruffles around her neck. His hands shook badly as they moved out toward the coral buttons, but by the time he had undone the third, his strong fingers were working with their customary deftness. The jade buttons of her skirt yielded as readily. Matthew, who knew from his long studious perusals of magazine advertisements that all girls wore pantyhose, was amazed and then intrigued that she had separate stockings and a garter belt. He noted for future reference in the Game that that made seven separate articles of clothing, if you counted shoes. With some difficulty he recalled his main purpose in all this. His hands edged under her long black curving hair until his middle fingers touched her burning ears.

He softly said, "The seven natural orifices of the *female* body, madam."

"What?" Her eyes blinked open wide and searched his face. Then a comic light flashed in them, though Matthew did not recognize it as such. Saying, "Oh, very well, sir. Go on," she closed them and renewed her blush. Matthew delicately touched her neat nostrils and her lips, then his right hand moved down while his eyes paused, marveling in admiration, at the two coral-tipped crucial points of a girl embellished on Severeign's chest.

"Seven," he finished triumphantly, amazed at his courage while lost in wonder at the newness of it all.

Her hands lightly clasped his shoulders, she leaned her head against his and whispered in his ear, "No, eight. You missed one." Her hand went down and her fingers instructed his. It was true! Matthew felt himself flushing furiously from intellectual shame. He'd known *that* about girls, of course, and yet he'd had a blind spot. There was a strange difference, he had to admit, between things read about in books of human physiology and things that were concretely there, so you could touch them. Severeign reminded him he still owed the Game a seven, and in his fluster he gave her the seven crucial points of a girl, which she was inclined to allow, though only by making an exception, for as she pointed out, they seemed very much Matthew's private thing, though possibly others had hit on them independently.

Still deeply mortified by his fundamental oversight, though continuing to be intensely interested in everything (the loose electricity lingered on him), Matthew would not accept the favor. "The Seven Wise Men of Greece—Solon, Thales, and so on," he said loudly and somewhat angrily, betting himself that those old boys had made a lot of slips in their time.

She nodded absently, and looking somewhat smugly down herself, said (quite fatuously, Matthew thought), "The seven seals on the Book of the Lamb."

He said more loudly, his strange anger growing, "In the Civil War, the Battle of Seven Pines, also called the Battle of Fair Oaks."

She looked at him, raised an eyebrow, and said, "The Seven Maxims of the Seven Wise Men of Greece." She looked down herself again and then down and up him. Her eyes, merry, met his. "Such as Pittacus: *Know thy opportunity*."

Matthew said still more loudly, "The Seven Days Battles, also Civil War, June twenty-fifth to July first inclusive, 1862—Mechanicsville, et cetera!"

She winced at the noise. "You've got to the fourth age now," she told him.

42

"What are you talking about?" he demanded.

"You know, Shakespeare. You gave it: the Seven Ages of Man. Fourth: 'Then a soldier, full of strange oaths and bearded like the pard, jealous in honor, sudden and quick in quarrel, seeking the bubble reputation even in the cannon's mouth.' You haven't got a beard, but you're roaring like a cannon."

"I don't care. You watch out. What's your seven?"

She continued to regard herself demurely, her eyes half closed. "Seven swans a-swimming," she said liltingly and a dancing vibration seemed to move down her white body, like that which goes out from a swan across the still surface of a summer lake.

Matthew roared, "The Seven Sisters, meaning the Scotch cannon at the Battle of Flodden!"

She shrugged maddeningly and murmured, "Sweet Seventeen," again giving herself the once-over.

"That's Sixteen," he shouted. "And it's not even a seven anyhow!"

She wrinkled her nose at him, turned her back, and said smiling over her shoulder, "Chilon: *Consider the end.*" And she jounced her little rump.

In his rage Matthew astonished himself by reaching her in a stride, picking her up like a feather, and dropping her in the middle of the bed, where she continued to smile self-infatuatedly as she bounced.

He stood glaring down at her and taking deep breaths preparatory to roaring, but then he realized his anger had disappeared.

"The Seven Hells," he said anticlimactically.

She noticed him, rolled over once and lay facing him on her side, chin in hand. "The seven virtues," she said. "Prudence, justice, temperance, and fortitude—those are Classical—and faith, hope and charity—those are Christian."

He lay down facing her. "The seven sins—"

43

"We've had those," she cut him off. "You gave them last night."

He at once remembered everything about the incident except the embarrassment.

"*Seven Footprints to Satan,* a novel by Abraham Merritt," he said, eyeing her with interest and idly throwing out an arm.

"*The Seven-Year Itch,* a film with Marilyn Monroe," she countered, doing likewise. Their fingers touched.

He rolled over toward her, saying, "*Seven Conquests,* a book by Poul Anderson," and ended up with his face above hers. He kissed her. She kissed him. In the starlight her face seemed to him that of a young goddess. And in the even, tranquil, shameless voice such a supernatural being would use, she said, "The seven stages of loving intercourse. First kissing. Then foreplay." After a while, "Penetration," and with a wicked starlit smile, "Bias: *Most men are bad.* Say a seven."

"Why?" Matthew asked, almost utterly lost in what they were doing, because it was endlessly new and heretofore utterly unimaginable to him—which was a very strange concept for a mathematician.

"So I can say one, stupid."

"Oh, very well. The seven spots to kiss: ears, eyes, cheeks, mouth," he said, suiting actions to words.

"How very specialized a seven. Try eyebrow flutters, too," she suggested, demonstrating. "But it will do for an answer in the Game. The seven gaits in running the course you're into. First the walk. Slowly, slowly. No, more slowly." After a while, she said, "Now the amble, not much faster. Shakespeare made it the slowest gait of Time, when he moves at all. Leisurely, stretchingly. Yes, that's right," and after a while, "Now the pace. In a horse, which is where all this comes from, that means first the hoofs on the one side, then those on the other. Right, left, right, see?—only doubled. There's a swing to it. Things are picking up." After a while she said, "Now the trot. I'll tell you who Time trots withal. Marry, he trots hard with a maid between the contract of her marriage and the day it is solemnized. A little harder. There, that's right." After a while she said, gasping slightly, "Now the canter. Just for each seventh instant we've all hoofs off the ground. Can you feel that? Yes, there it came again. Press on." After a while she said, gasping, "And now the rack. That's six gaits. Deep penetration too. Which makes five stages. Oh, press on." Matthew felt he was being tortured on a rack, but the pain was wonderful, each frightening moment an utterly new revelation. After a while she gasped, "Now, sir, the gallop!"

Matthew said, gasping too, "Is this wise, madam? Won't we come apart? Where are you taking me? Recall Cleobulus: *Avoid Excess!*"

But she cried ringingly, her face lobster-red, "No, it's not sane, it's mad! But we must run the risk. To the heights and above! To the ends of the earth and beyond! Press on, press on, the Game is all! Epimenides: *Nothing is impossible to industry!*" After a while he redded out.

After another while he heard her say, remotely, tenderly, utterly without effort, "Last scene of all, that ends this strange, eventful history, is mere oblivion. Now Time stands still withal. After the climax—sixth stage—there is afterplay. What's your seven?"

He answered quite as dreamily, "The Seven Heavens, abodes of bliss to the Mohammedans and cabalists."

She said, "That's allowable, although you gave it once before by inference. The seven syllables of the basic hymn line, as 'Hark, the herald angels sing.'"

45

He echoed with, "Join the triumph of the skies."

She said, "Look at the stars." He did. She said, "Look how the floor of heaven is thick inlaid with patens of bright gold." It was.

He said, "There's not the smallest orb which thou behold'st but in his motion like an angel sings. Hark." She did.

Math felt the stars were almost in his head. He felt they were the realm in which he'd lived in infancy and that with a tiny effort he could at this very moment push across the border and live there again. What was so wrong about Pythagoreanism? Weren't numbers real, if you could live among them? And wouldn't they be alive and have personalities, if they were everything there was? Something most strange was happening.

Severeign nodded, then pointed a finger straight up. "Look, the Pleiades. I always thought they were the Little Dipper. They'd hit us in our tummies if they fell."

He said, gazing at them, "You've already used that seven."

"Of course I have," she said, still dreamily. "I was just making conversation. It's your turn, anyway."

He said, "Of course. The Philosophical Pleiad, another name for the Seven Wise Men of Greece."

She said, "The Alexandrian Pleiad—Homer the younger and six other poets."

He said, "The French Pleiad—Ronsard and his six."

She said, "The Pleiades again, meaning the seven nymphs, attendant on Diana, for whom the stars were named—Alcyone, Celaeno, Electra, Maia (she's Illusion), Taygete (she got lost), Sterope (she wed war) and Merope (she married Sisyphus). My, that got gloomy."

Matthew looked down from the stars and fondly at her, counting over her personal and private sevens.

"What's the matter?" she asked.

46

"Nothing," he said. Actually, he'd winced at the sudden memory of his eight-orifices error. The recollection faded back as he continued to study her.

"The Seven Children of the Days of the Week, Fair-of-Face and Full-of-Grace, and so on," he said, drawing out the syllables. "Whose are you?"

"Saturday's—"

"Then you've got far to go," he said.

She nodded, somewhat solemnly.

"And that makes another seven that belongs to you," he added. "The seventh day of the week."

"No, sixth," she said. "Sunday's the seventh day of the week."

"No, it's the first," he told her with a smile. "Look at any calendar." He felt a lazy pleasure at having caught her out, though it didn't make up for a Game error like the terrible one he'd made.

She said, " 'The Seven Ravens,' a story by the Brothers Grimm. Another gloomy one."

He said, gazing at her and speaking as if they too belonged to her, "The Seven Wonders of the World. The temple of Diana at Ephesus, et cetera. Say, what's the matter?"

She said, "You said the World when we were in the Stars. It brought me down. The world's a nasty place."

"I'm sorry, Sev," he said. "You are a goddess, did you know? I saw it when the starlight freckled you. Diana coming up twice in the Game reminded me. Goddesses are supposed to be up in the stars, like in line drawings of the constellations with stars in their knees and heads."

"The world's a nasty place," she repeated. "Its number's nine."

"I thought six sixty-six," he said. "The number of the beast. Somewhere in Revelations."

"That too," she said, "but mostly nine."

47

"The smallest odd number that is not a prime," he said.

"The number of the Dragon. Very nasty. Here, I'll show you just how nasty."

She dipped over the edge of the bed for her purse and put in his hands something that felt small, hard, cold and complicated. Then, kneeling upright on the bed, she reached out and switched on the lamps.

Matthew lunged past her and hit the switch for the ceiling drapes.

"Afraid someone might see us?" she asked as the drapes rustled toward each other.

He nodded mutely, catching his breath through his nose. Like her, he was now kneeling upright on the bed.

"The stars are far away," she said. "Could they see us with telescopes?"

"No, but the roof is close," he whispered back. "Though it's unlikely anyone would be up there."

Nevertheless he waited, watching the ceiling, until the drapes met and the faint whirring stopped. Then he looked at what she'd put in his hands.

He did not drop it, but he instantly shifted his fingers so that he was holding it with a minimum of contact between his skin and it, very much as a man would hold a large dark spider which for some occult reason he may not drop.

It was a figurine, in blackened bronze or else in some dense wood, of a fearfully skinny, wiry old person tautly bent over backward like a bow, knees somewhat bent, arms straining back overhead. The face was witchy, nose almost meeting pointed chin across toothlessly grinning gums pressed close together, eyes bulging with mad evil. What seemed at first some close-fitting, ragged garment was then seen to be only loathsomely diseased skin, here starting to peel, there showing pustules, open ulcers, and other tetters, all

48

worked in the metal (or carved in even harder wood) in abominably realistic miniscule detail. Long empty dugs hanging back up the chest as far as the neck made it female, but the taut legs, somewhat spread, showed a long flaccid penis caught by the artificer in extreme swing to the left, and far back from it a long grainy scrotum holding shriveled testicles caught in similar swing to the right, and in the space between them long leprous vulva gaping.

"It's nasty, isn't it?" Severeign said dryly of the hideous hermaphrodite. "My Aunt Helmintha bought it in Crotona, that one-time Greek colony in the instep of the Italian Boot where Pythagoras was born—bought it from a crafty old dealer in antiquities, who said it came from 'Earth's darkest center' by way of Mali and North Africa. He said it was a figure of the World, a nine-thing, *Draco homo*. He said it can't be broken, must not, in fact, for if you break it, the world will disappear or else you and those with you will forever vanish—no one knows where."

Staring at the figurine, Math muttered, "The seven days and nights the Ancient Mariner saw the curse in the dead man's eye."

She echoed, "The seven days and nights his friends sat with Job."

He said, his shoulders hunched, "The Seven Words, meaning the seven utterances of Christ on the cross."

She said, "The seven gates to the land of the dead through which Ishtar passed."

He said, his shoulders working, "The seven golden vials full of the wrath of God that the four beasts gave to the seven angels."

She said, shivering a little, "The birds known as the Seven Whistlers and considered to be a sign of some great calamity impending." Then, "Stop it, Math!"

Still staring at the figurine, he had shifted his grip on

49

it, so that his thick forefingers hooked under its knees and elbows while his big thumbs pressed against its arched narrow belly harder and harder. But at her command his hands relaxed and he returned the thing to her purse.

"Fie on you, sir!" she said, "to try to run out on the Game, and on me, and on yourself. The seven letters in Matthew, and in Fortree. Remember Solon: *Know thyself*."

He answered, "The fourteen letters in Sovereign Saxon, making two sevens too."

"The seven syllables in Master Matthias Fortree," she said, flicking off the lamps before taking a step toward him on her knees.

"The seven syllables in Mamsel Sovereign Saxon," he responded, putting his arms around her.

And then he was murmuring, "Oh Sovereign, my sovereign," and they were both wordlessly indicating sevens they'd named earlier, beginning with the seven crucial points of a girl ("Crucial green points," he said, and "Of a green girl," said she), and the whole crucial part of the evening was repeated, only this time it extended endlessly with infinite detail, although all he remembered of the Game from it was her saying "The Dance of the Seven Veils," and him replying "The seven figures in the Dance of Death as depicted on a hilltop by Ingmar Bergman in his film," and her responding, "The Seven Sleepers of Ephesus," and him laboriously getting out, "In the like legend in the Koran, the seven sleepers guarded by the dog Al Rakim," and her murmuring, "Good doggie, good doggie," as he slowly, slowly, sank into bottomless slumber.

Next morning Math woke to blissful dreaminess instead of acutely stabbing misery for the first time in his life since he had lost his childhood power to live wholly in the world of numbers. Strong sunlight was seeping through the ceiling. Severeign was gone with all her things, including the purse with its disturbing figurine, but that did not bother him in the least (nor did his eight-error, the only other possible flyspeck on his paradise), for he knew with absolute certainty that he would see her again that evening. He dressed himself and went out into the corridor and wandered along it until he saw from the corner of his eye that he was strolling alongside Elmo Hooper, whereupon he poured out to that living memory bank all his joy, every detail of last night's revelations.

As he ended his long litany of love, he noticed bemusedly that Elmo had dropped back, doubtless because they were overtaking three theoretical physicists headed for the Commons. Their speech had a secretive tone, so he tuned his ears to it and was soon in possession of a brand-new top secret they did well to whisper about, and they none the wiser—a secret that just might allow him to retrieve his eight-error, he realized with a throb of superadded happiness. (In fact, he was so happy he even thought on the spur of the moment of a second string for that bow.)

So when Severeign came that night, as he'd known she would, he was ready for her. Craftily he did not show his cards at first, but when she began with, "The Seven Sages, those male Scheherazades who night after night keep a king from putting his son wrongfully to death," he followed her lead with "The Seven Wise Masters, another name for the Seven Sages."

She said, "The Seven Questions of Timur the Lame—Tamurlane."

He said, "The Seven Eyes of Ningauble."

"Pardon?"

"Never mind. *Seven Men* (including 'Enoch Soames' and 'A. V. Laider'), a book of short stories by Max Beerbohm."

She said, "*The Seven Pillars of Wisdom*, a book by Lawrence of Arabia."

He said, "*The Seven Faces of Dr. Lao,* a fantasy film."

She said, "Just *The Seven Faces* by themselves, a film Paul Muni starred in."

He said, "The seven Gypsy jargons mentioned by Borrow in his *Bible in Spain.*"

She said, "*Seven Brides for Seven Brothers,* another film."

He said, "The dance of the seven veils—how did we miss it?"

She said, "Or miss the seven stars in the hair of the blessed damosel?"

He said, "Or the Seven Hills of San Francisco when we got Rome's?"

She said, "*Seven Keys to Baldpate*, a play by George M. Cohan."

He said, "*Seven Famous Novels*, an omnibus by H. G. Wells."

She said, "*The Seven That Were Hanged,* a novella by Andreyev."

That's my grim cue, he thought, but I'll try my second string first. "The seven elements whose official names begin with N, and their symbols," he said, and then recited rapidly, poker-faced, "N for Nitrogen, Nb for Nobelium, Nd for Neodymium, Ne for Neon, Ni for Nickel, No for Niobrium, Np for Neptunium."

She grinned fiendishly, started to speak, then caught herself. Her eyes widened at him. Her grin changed, though not much.

"Matthew, you rat!" she said. "You wanted me to correct you, say there were eight and that you'd missed Na. But then I'd have been in the wrong, for Na is for Sodium—its old and unofficial name Natrium."

Math grinned back at her, still poker-faced, though

his confidence had been shaken. Nevertheless he said, "Quit stalling. What's your seven?"

She said, *"The Seven Lamps of Architecture*, a book of essays by John Ruskin."

He said, baiting his trap, "The seven letters in the name of the radioactive element Pluton—I mean Uranium."

She said, "That's feeble, sir. All words with seven letters would last almost forever. But you've made me think of a very good one, entirely legitimate. The seven isotopes of Plutonium and Uranium, sum of their Pleiades."

"Huh! I got you, madam," he said, stabbing a finger at her.

Her face betrayed exasperation of a petty sort, but then an entirely different sort of consternation, almost panic fear.

"You're wrong, madam," he said triumphantly. "There are, as I learned only today—"

"Stop!" she cried. "Don't say it! You'll be sorry! Remember Thales: *Suretyship is the precursor of ruin.*"

He hesitated a moment. He thought, that means don't cosign checks. Could that be stretched to mean don't share dangerous secrets? No, too far-fetched.

"You won't escape being shown up that easily," he said gleefully. "There are *eight* isotopes now, as I learned only this morning. Confess yourself at fault."

He stared at her eagerly, triumphantly, but only saw her face growing pale. Not ashamed, not exasperated, not contumacious even, but fearful. Dreadfully fearful.

There were three rapid, very loud knocks on the door.

They both started violently.

The knocks were repeated, followed by a bellow that penetrated all soundproofing. "Open up in there!" it boomed hollowly. "Come on out, Fortree! *And* the girl."

53

Matthew goggled. Severeign suddenly dug in her purse and tossed him something. It was the figurine.

"Break it!" she commanded. "It's our only chance of escape."

He stared at it stupidly.

There was a ponderous pounding on the door, which groaned and crackled.

"Break it!" she cried. "Night before last you prayed. I brought the answer to your prayer. You have it in your hands. It takes us to your lost world that you loved. Break it, I say!"

A kind of comprehension came to Math's face. He hooked his fingers round the figure's evil ends, pressed on the arching loathsome midst.

"Who is your brother, Severeign?" he asked.

"You are my brother, in the other realm," she said. "Press, press!—and break the thing!"

The door began visibly to give under the strokes, now thunderous. The cords in Math's neck stood out, and the veins in his forehead; his knuckles grew white.

"Break it for me," she cried. "For Severeign! *For Seven!*"

The sound of the door bursting open masked a lesser though sharper crack. Warren Dean and his party plunged into the room to find it empty, and no one in the bedroom or bathroom either.

It had been he, of course, whom Matthew, utterly bemused, had mistaken for Elmo Hooper that morning. Dean had immediately reactivated the bugs in Matthew's apartment. It is from their record that this account of Matthew's and Severeign's last night is reconstructed. All the rest of the story derives from the material overheard by Dean (who quite obviously, from this narrative, has his own Achilles' heel) or retrieved from Elmo Hooper.

The case is still very open, of course. That fact alone

has made the Coexistence Complex an even more uneasy place than before—something that most connoisseurs of its intrigues had deemed impossible. The theory of security is the dread one that Matthew Fortree was successfully spirited away to one of the hostiles by the diabolical spy Severeign Saxon. By what device remains unknown, although the walls of the Coexistence Complex have been systematically burrowed through in search of secret passageways more thoroughly than even termites could have achieved, without discovering anything except several lost bugging systems.

A group of daring thinkers believes that Matthew, on the basis of his satanic mathematical cunning and his knowledge of the eighth isotope of the uranium-plutonium pair, and probably with technological knowhow from behind some iron curtain supplied by Severeign, devised an innocent-looking mechanism, which was in fact a matter transmitter, by means of which they escaped to the country of Severeign's employers. All sorts of random setups were made of Matthew's ivories. Their investigation became a sort of hobby-in-itself for some and led to several games and quasi-religious cults, and to two suicides.

Others believe Severeign's employers were extraterrestrial. But a rare few quietly entertain the thought and perhaps the hope that hers was a farther country than that even, that she came from the Pythagorean universe where Matthew spent much of his infancy and early childhood, the universe where numbers are real and one can truly fall in love with Seven, briefly incarnate as a Miss S.S.

Whatever the case, Matthew Fortree and Severeign Saxon are indeed gone, vanished without a trace or clue except for a remarkably nasty figurine showing a fresh, poisonously green surface where it was snapped in two, which is the only even number that is a prime.

Human history is, among other things, the story of continual improvement in the quality of life, as science has given us greater creature comforts, longer life spans, increasing range in travel and communications. But it's possible that we've passed our zenith, for unless we develop new and safe sources of energy, our technological civilization cannot be maintained at its present level and our descendants may be forced back to more primitive modes of life.

Brian Aldiss has written before of the downfall of civilization, in such novels as **Greybeard** and **Earthworks,** but in the following tale he reminds us that different people have contrasting responses to change. What, after all, determines the quality of anyone's life?

MY LADY OF THE PSYCHIATRIC SORROWS

Brian W. Aldiss

Goddard worked with the northern reindeer herds all that long winter. With the other skin-clad men, he followed the migratory pattern of the animals in their search for lichens through snow or shine. He slept by beggarly fires under pines or under the stars. His whole life was encompassed by the sad guilts in reindeer eyes, by clouds of reindeer breath hanging in the crisp air.

The herd consisted of some hundred thousand

beasts. They moved in good mild order, with their attendant pest-army of mosquitoes and bloodsucking flies. Their antlers appeared like a moving forest.

For Goddard, it was a Pleistocene way of life. But when spring came he was paid off and began to walk south, back to Scally and the children, with his dog Gripp at his side.

He walked for sixteen days, steadily. The climate grew warmer. The steaks in his pack began to stink, but still he ate them. Every now and then, he came to villages or mills; always he avoided them.

At last, he was among the vales of the Gray Horse. He walked through sparse forests, where the beech, birch, and hazel bushes were putting forth green leaves. Through the trees, standing by the old highway, was his home. His father was working in the garden. Goddard called to him, and the guard dogs, Chase and Setter, started furious barking.

"How are the children?" Goddard asked his father, embracing the old man. His father was still upright, though the winter months seemed to have shrunk him.

"Come and see. They aren't half growing big!"

"You've made out?"

"Fine, Tom. And I've not heard of a case of plague all winter."

"Good."

"It'll mean that people will be coming back. . . ."
As they spoke, they walked together, close, to the rear of the house, where the windmill stood on the rise above their small stream. Gripp kept to Goddard's heel.

The children were there—Derek wading in the stream, June kneeling on the bank. Both were picking reeds. They dropped them and ran with cries of delight into their father's embrace. He rolled on the ground with them, all three of them laughing and crying.

57

"You don't half smell animal, Dad!"

"I've been an animal. . . ." He was proud of them, both so big and strong, neither older than seven, their eyes clear, their glance candid—as their mother's once had been.

Granddad roasted one of the rotting steaks and they all ate, throwing gristle and bone to the dogs. After, Goddard slept in a downstairs room. He woke once. The sun had gone. His father and the children were in the other room, weaving hurdles from willow sticks by the light of two candles. They called to him affectionately; but when he had urinated outside, he staggered back to his cot and slept again.

In the morning they swarmed over him once more. He kissed and hugged them, and they screamed at his rough lips and beard.

"It's a holiday today. What shall we do?"

"Go and see Mother, of course. Let's feed the animals first."

The goat, the two sows, the chickens, the rabbits, were fed. Leaving the dogs on guard, they all set out along the vale to see Mother. The children snatched up sticks from ditches, leaning heavily on them and saying in their clear voices, "Now we are *old* children." Their laughter seemed to settle about Goddard's heart.

A stramineous sun broke through the mists. Where the track turned, they saw the bulk of the planetoid ahead, and the children set up a muted cheer.

Goddard said to his father, turning from that shadow-shrouded form, "I don't reckon I could bear life without the kids and all their happiness. I dread when they'll turn into adults and go their way."

"It'll be different then. Don't look ahead." But the old man turned his head away sorrowfully.

"They seem to have a purpose, over and above keeping alive—just like the reindeer."

His father had no answer.

The planetoid was so immense that it blocked the valley. It had created its own ecoclimate. On this side, the northern side, dark hardy bushes had grown at its base, rock and stone had piled up, and a stream dashed from it. The top of the planetoid's shell showed serrated through thinning cloud.

Derek and June dropped back in awe. June took her father's hand. "Don't it look huge this morning! Tell us how it came here, Dad."

They always liked the drama of the old story. Goddard said, "As the reindeer roam in search of food, men used to roam in search of energy. When the local supplies ran out, they built a mass of little planets, like this one, called zeepees. The zeepees circled about in space, getting energy from the sun. But some of the planetoids got in trouble, just like people. This one—I think it was called Fragrance, or something fancy—it crashed here. Another one went into the sun. Another one drifted off toward the stars."

"Was that years and years ago, Dad?" Derek asked. He took up a stone and flung it, to show he was not scared.

"Not so long ago. Only, let's see, only six years ago. The zeepee was empty by then. All the people in it had come back to Earth, so nobody was hurt."

"Did Mother go to live there as soon as it crashed?"

"After a bit, yes."

They climbed up a steeply winding path to one side, where the soil had been flung back by the impact. Broom and nettles grew now. The enormous hull was plastic. Its fall through the atmosphere had caused blisters to erupt, so that its sides were warted and striped like a toad.

"I bet it came down with a great big CRASH!" June said.

"It split right open like an egg," her granddad told her.

Goddard led them in through the broken hatch, going cautiously. There had been looting at first. Now all was deserted.

The children fell silent as they walked. The amazing, jumbled maze which had once been a city, a world, was no longer lit, except by daylight filtering in through the ruptured hull. They walked not on floors and roads but on sides of tunnels and walls of corridors. The stress of impact had caused fractures and crazy distortions of the structure. Defunct lights and signs sprouted underfoot. Doorways had become hatches leading to dry wells. Once-busy intersections produced shafts leading up into nothingness. Dummies stared down at them from overhead tanks which had been shop windows. They tramped across the hitherto inaccessible, where stairways had become abstract bas-reliefs.

"It's cold—I shouldn't like to live here," June said. "Not unless I was a polar bear."

They waded through a riverlet. Cracked and broken, the planetoid lay open to the elements. The rains of autumn, the snows of winter, all blew in among Fragrance's complex structures, turning yesterday's apartments into today's reservoirs. Slowly the water leaked downward through the upturned city, draining at last into native ground. Plants and fungi were getting a grasp on ruined precincts. Small animals had taken over the defunct sewage system. Sparrows and starlings built their nests in what had once been an underground railway, several thousand miles above Earth. After the birds came smaller life forms. Flies and spiders and wasps and beetles and moths. Change worked at everything. What had been impregnable to the rigors of space fell to the ardors of a mild spring.

"Dad, why does Mother want to live here?" Derek asked.

"She liked the old times. She couldn't take to the new."

Goddard never forgot the way to the spot where Scally had settled in. She had indulged her sybaritic tastes and ensconced herself in what had been Fragrance's chief hotel, the Astral. Goddard had found only one way of entering the hotel, which had stood in a block on its own, and that was by way of a metal ladder which an early looter had propped up against a fire exit overhead. Goddard leading, the four of them climbed the ladder and worked their way into the foyer, whose elaborate reception area now projected from one wall. Loose debris had provided the wall on which they stood with a carpet.

Scally had barricaded herself into the old bar. They climbed up a pile of tumbled desks, calling her name through the shattered doors.

He remembered the dirty tomblike smell of her lair. The smell of dead hope, he told himself.

In her first year here, Goddard had come up often from the Vale of the Gray Horse—for sex, for love, or for pity. Scally had not wanted the outside world, and had slowly, almost against her own will, rejected him as a symbol of it. He had helped her make herself comfortable here. So she lived in aspic, in dowdy magnificence, the great cracked mirrors of her ceiling reflecting every torpid move she made.

As her husband and children appeared, she rose from a chair. Instead of coming toward them, she retreated to the far wall. She was tall and soft; the last few indoor years had turned her all gray. As she smiled at them, a long pallid hand crept up to cover her lips.

"Mother, look, Dad's back from the North!" Derek said, running over and clutching her, making her bend over and kiss him and June. "He's been with reindeer."

"You're getting so big and rough," Scally said, letting go of them and backing away, until she could lean against a piano in a self-conscious attitude.

Conscious of his coarse skins, Goddard went over and took her in his arms. She was thinner and drier than previously, while all around her compartments bulged with the rich damps of decay. Her expression as she searched his face wounded him.

"It's spring again, Scally," he said. "Come out with us. Come home. We'll fix the roof, Dad and I, and get one of the upstairs rooms done specially for you."

"This is my place," she said.

"The children need you." But the children had lost interest in their mother, and were questing about the room and adjacent corridors. They had found two rods to walk with; June was laughing and calling, "Now we're a couple of old children again!"

"I'm a hundred years old."

"I'm a thousand and sixty hundred years old."

"I'm even older than Mum."

Goddard's father was embarrassed. He looked about and eventually left the room too, to follow the children.

"He hates me!" Scally said, pointing at the closing door.

"No, he doesn't. He just doesn't have anything to say. He hates this prison."

"He thinks I should come back and look after you and the children."

"Why don't you? We need you. You could take some of this furniture."

"Huh! I'd only be a liability to you."

"Scally, you're my wife. I'd gladly have you back. This place is no good. Why do you stay here?"

She looked away, waved a hand in dismissal. "You ask such fool questions."

Angry, he grasped her wrist. "Come on, then, we take the trouble to come and see you! Tell me why you want to live in this muddy ruin, come on—tell me!"

Through the dim upturned light, a glow crept into her features. "Because I can't take reality the way you can! You're so stupidly insensitive, you don't mind the beastly pig-reality of the present. But some of us live by myth, by legend. Just as the children do, until you turn them out of it and make them grow up before their time."

He said sullenly, "You only came here because you thought you'd be a bit more comfortable. It's nothing to do with myth."

"While I'm here, I'm in the remains of an age when men lived by their myths, when they created machines and looked outward, when they didn't wallow in every muddy season and grovel on the ground as you do! This room once sailed among the stars—and all you can imagine is that I'm after comfort."

She laughed bitterly.

Goddard scratched his head. "I know it's kind of uncomfortable back at home. But honest, if you can face up to it, life's better than it used to be in the old days. It's more real. Less of all that waffle, all those things we didn't really need."

She folded her arms, no longer looking as faded as she had five minutes earlier. "You were born to be a farmer, Tom, to walk behind cattle and reindeer, tramping through their droppings. Of course you rejoice at the death of the consumer society. But that wasn't all we had, was it? Remember the other things the Catastrophe killed off? The hope that we were moving toward a better world, the feeling that mankind might come to some sort of ethical maturity as he left his home planet? I resent being kicked back into the Dark Ages, if you don't."

He did not know what to say. He shook his head. "Resentment's no way to shape your life."

"There *is* no shape to life, Tom. Not any more. Style died along with everything else. Why, when I look at you . . ." She turned away. "To think you were a top sports-clothes designer! In six years you've become nothing but a peasant."

The children were screaming with feigned terror in one of the upside-down corridors.

"I'll try and make you comfortable if you come home," Goddard said. She could always confuse him. Half aware that he was only infuriating her, he put out a hand pleadingly, but she turned away toward the table and chair at which she had been sitting when they entered.

"At least I can read here, at least my mind is free." She had picked a book up from the table.

He shook his head. "All that old world is dead and gone, my dear. Books are where you get your sick notions from. Throw it away and come into the light of day. The plague has gone and things'll be better."

The children were screaming with delight outside.

"Today or yesterday, I was reading about the scientific basis for the legend of the Golden Fleece," Scally told Goddard. "Did you ever hear of the Greek legend of the Golden Fleece, and how Jason and the Argonauts went in search of it? The story has always related to the Black Sea area. When this book was published, researchers had analyzed pieces of cloth from the tomb of an old king of that area, Tumulus I, who lived in the Fifth Century, B.C. That was the period of Jason and his crew. Do you know what the researchers found?"

He tried to escape from the conversation, but she went on remorselessly, although the children had come back hooting into the room.

"They found that the cloth from the tomb was composed of extremely fine fibers, with mean diameters of—I forget the exact measurements—about sixteen micrometers, I believe. That is the earliest appearance of true fine-wooled sheep by several centuries. So you see that all that golden legend was generated by Jason and his friends going in search of more comfortable underwear." She laughed.

The children had tied sticks around their heads with old fabric.

"Look, Dad, Mother! We're reindeer. We've gone wild! We're going to head north and we'll never let anyone milk us again!"

Puzzled by her story, Goddard said to her over the racket, "I don't understand you properly. Whatever happened to those Argonauts can't affect us, can it?"

She looked at him wearily, with her eyelids lowered. "Take these young reindeer away," she said. "One day soon their myths will break down. Don't you see, there's a prosaic reality to every legend, but people like you beat legends into prosaic reality."

"I never beat you!"

"Have you got remarkably thick in the head, or is that meant to be funny?"

"You're sick, Scally, really you are. Come away and let me look after you!"

"Never say that again! You oaf, if you didn't believe that I was sick, can't you see that I might come with you willingly?"

Goddard scratched his head. "Since you can always get the better of me in words, I can't think why you're afraid to come with me." Then he turned away.

The next day was mild and springlike. Goddard stripped to the waist and began to plant row after row of seed potatoes, which his father had carefully cherished throughout the winter. The two children played on the other side of the stream, building little planetoids in every bush, and pretending that Gripp was a monster from outer space.

Here's a story about a bar infested with gremlins—
so that means it's a fantasy, right? Well, maybe
not: it's also about the interface between alternate
time-streams, a most respectable science fiction
idea. Mainly, it's an ingenious and funny story,
which is the definition that **really** counts.

Probability Storm is Julian Reid's first published
story. Born in London, he earned a B.A. in English
and Philosophy at the University of Victoria and
attended the first Clarion SF Writers' Workshop
in Seattle, where he "had a story (literally) torn to
pieces by Harlan Ellison" and was involved with
Samuel R. Delany in plotting the never-to-be-written
adventures of Lust Hog, the Ultimate Male Chau-
vinist Pig. Considering this somewhat mad atmosphere, it isn't surprising that the idea for **Probability
Storm** came to Reid during that workshop.

PROBABILITY STORM

Julian Reid

If you've never been to Rafferty's, you won't believe
a word of this—I'm warning you right off, because dis-
believing can be dangerous. Look what happened to
Howard Hopper and General Wilbur Prescott and
Lady Beatrice Annabelle Scraggs; you've heard of
them, I'm sure. Or remember how dynasties used to
topple when Edward Everett Peaslake let his mind
wander, and how the Dow-Jones Average dropped

thirteen whole points the day Isadora Edison discovered a minor compositor's error at the bottom of the third column on page forty-three of the Sunday *New York Times*. And then there was the infamous Barnabas Tobin with his terrible Exopsychic Deontologizer, which was on the verge of reducing the entire world to a state of primordial chaos by the time the Duly Constituted Authorities belatedly intervened. There are things I could tell you about Barnabas Tobin . . . but I'd better not. After all, a word to the wise is sufficient.

So maybe, before you read the rest of this, you ought to drop in at Rafferty's. Tonight, if you can make it; or if you can't, tomorrow at the very latest. You'll have no difficulty finding the place: just drive north on Twenty-ninth until you come to the big wrought-iron gates of the North American Institute of Parapsychic Technology. Then slow down and shift to the outside lane, if you aren't in it already. It's only another three blocks, and then you swing right onto Washington Avenue—which is named after *the* Washington, George Henry I mean, the man who invented the Transcendental Impulsifier. Keep going for two more blocks and you're there.

The sign over the entrance is small and tastefully discreet, but you can't possibly miss it if you have your eyes open and your wits about you. It reads *"Rafferty's* WHY NOT? *Tavern,"* and the "WHY NOT?" is in Old Gothic Black-letter while the rest is in flowing Spencerian script. The words are carved into a varnished slab of Oregon cedar, which is said to come from the very tree that Rafferty's grandfather chopped down a century ago in order to release the dryad who later became his wife. It's illuminated from below by two small spotlights which have been burning steadily for twenty-seven years now, ever since the day Rafferty and his bride Moira first took over the establishment.

Rafferty screwed in one bulb and Moira the other, and they both together pulled the switch that made the power flow. Some say there's magic in those lights, but there isn't—you have my word for that. What makes them glow is electricity, and there's nothing magical about electricity.

Anyway, as I said before, you can't possibly miss the place—unless, of course, there are gremlins around. But you know how gremlins are, and you're in a pretty sad state if you haven't learned yet how to get on with them. Just be patient and keep your wits about you, and above all don't lose your temper—if you don't let them ruffle you, they'll tire of the game soon enough. Still, maybe I should warn you that if you're one of those smug, stuffy types who can't stand gremlins, you'd best stay away from Rafferty's. There's usually a whole crowd of them in the neighborhood, you see; they seem to like the place. Myself, I'm glad they do; I'd be pretty lonely without them. But that's an opinion you're not obligated to share.

So anyway, now you're at Rafferty's, and there's not much point in having gone that far unless you stop and go inside. Fortunately, parking is no problem; the City has seen to that. There are meters all down the street, both sides, and you shouldn't have much trouble finding one that isn't full yet and paying to have your car dematerialized for as long as you plan to stay. Of course, sometimes the gremlins take it into their minds to interfere with the meters, so there's an off-chance that your spanking new Cadillac Eldorado might rematerialize as a cranky old Volkswagen Beetle. But it's only a very off-chance, and it won't happen unless one of them takes a personal dislike to you. And anyway, the loss will be covered by your insurance, if you've been sensible enough to take out one of those new policies that cover Acts of Gremlins as well as Acts of God.

And that's the last of my warnings, even though there are one or two other points I might perhaps have mentioned. But don't worry about them—they don't concern you, not unlesss you happen to be a white-headed man with a red beard or an illegitimate descendant of Oliver Cromwell or the thirteenth daughter of the seventh daughter of a thirteenth son. Which isn't likely, these days; and besides, if you *are* one of these things, you've already learned that you've got to tread carefully. If you hadn't, you'd never have managed to survive this long, as Charles Darwin made himself famous by pointing out.

So from this point on, you're on your own. Once you're inside Rafferty's, literally anything might happen—provided, of course, it's permitted by both the Laws of Nature and the Constitution of these United States of America, together with the rules Rafferty himself has laid down for the conduct of a decent, well-run establishment. Even the gremlins respect those; they know they'll be thrown out if they don't. There aren't many people who can say *No* to an obstreperous gremlin and make it stick, but Rafferty is one of them. It's his dryad ancestry, I suspect—that and his marriage to Moira. No one would want to offend Moira, not even a gremlin. And besides, Moira is the seventh daughter of a seventh daughter, and you know what *that* means.

Now, on this particular night I'm telling you about, it just so happened that there weren't any gremlins around—not at first, anyway. Rafferty was there, of course, and Moira was upstairs washing the dinner dishes, and Soleful Susie, the barmaid, was sitting in the rear booth with her feet up, resting, and amusing herself by tickling the tummy of James Clerk Maxwell, the cat. It was early in the evening, sevenish, and there were still only half a dozen customers in the place. Old John Edgar Harding, the retired professor of 'Pataphysics who used to head the department at Miskatonic, was sitting at one end of the bar, discoursing ponderously to Rafferty on his theory of the Unrequited Middle. At the other end Louella van Doren, a red-headed three-times-divorcee who writes a monthly column on Creative Marriage Management for *Fortune* magazine, was conversing animatedly with Isherwood Foster, a handsome stockbroker some twenty years younger than herself. In the center booth on the left was Bryon Wilcox, the Neo-Dadaist poet, who always insists that he doesn't come to Rafferty's in search of inspiration, as other poets might, but only to get stinking drunk. And finally, in the last-but-one booth on the right, were two of the young whiz kids from the North American Institute, engrossed in a game of three-dimensional chess. Their names were Spassky and Fischer—but they weren't the Spassky and Fischer you're thinking of, nor even their *doppelgangers,* but two different people entirely. It's just a coincidence that they were both chess players, so don't worry about it: these things happen sometimes, especially in Rafferty's.

And that's the lot—more or less, because *I* was there too, of course. But *I* don't count, not really, because I wasn't corporeally present. I seldom am; I come and go, you see. But don't let that bother you—*I* don't, not any more. I'm used to it by now.

So anyway, that's how things were when The Fat Man came in. I call him The Fat Man because you wouldn't be interested in his family name, not if you know what's good for you, and he wasn't the type you'd care to be on first-name terms with. All you need to know about him is that he was ugly-fat, with jowls

70

that oozed down the sides of his face like candle drippings. And he was mean, too—you could tell that just by looking at him. It's said that inside of every fat man there's a thin man crying to get out; well, the thin man inside of this one had been swallowed up entirely and he wasn't even screaming any more. You can't get any meaner than that; it's positively cannibalistic.

It goes without saying that The Fat Man wasn't a regular at Rafferty's—for one thing, the gremlins would never have stood for him; and for another, he wasn't the sort who'd survive for long with a whole passel of gremlins around. But it just so happened, as I've already told you, that there weren't any gremlins there, not just then. So The Fat Man waddled up to the bar, all sticky-pink and for now unmolested, and heaved himself up onto one of the stools and sat squinting around. When he spotted Rafferty he crooked his finger and called out: "Hey! How about some service, eh?" His voice was gruff and grunty, like all the rest of him.

So Rafferty came over and said, as politely as he could manage: "Well, sir, what can I do for you?"

"You can get me a drink," said The Fat Man. "And make it strong, hear?" He wiggled his finger as he spoke, like it was a stick he carried round with him to beat on helpless animals and children when they had the effrontery to cross his path.

"Yes, sir," said Rafferty. He didn't ask what kind of drink it was that The Fat Man wanted—like all good bartenders, Rafferty is prescient in these matters. And The Fat Man knew this; I'm not sure how, but he knew.

So Rafferty mixed up a double whiskey sour for him; and meantime The Fat Man sat squinting around piggily. "Nice place you got here," he said. "Funny I never noticed it before. Been here quite a while, from the looks of it."

"Twenty-seven years," said Rafferty.

"Now that's pee-cool-ier," said The Fat Man. "Twenty-seven years you been in this neighborhood, and I never noticed—not even once. Now that's what I call pee-cool-ier—*most* pee-cool-ier."

"It's been known to happen," said Rafferty, feeling obliged to comment. "Some people just ain't observant—you know how it is." He knew that it must be gremlins' work, of course; but he wasn't going to say that to The Fat Man's face—Rafferty is a great believer in Etiquette. "That'll be a buck twenty-five," he added, setting down the whiskey sour.

"You don't say," said The Fat Man, hauling out his wallet. "But take *me*, now," he went on, "I've always considered myself a pretty observant guy." He handed Rafferty a ten. "No sir, I don't make a habit of missing things, not me. I'd never of gotten where I am today if I hadn't of kept my eyes peeled all the way. Now this is a real nice place you got here—yes sir, it surely is. Does pretty good business, too, if I don't miss my bet."

"Not bad," said Rafferty, ringing up on the cash-register and counting out The Fat Man's change.

"Of course," said The Fat Man, "it *could* be better—now ain't that so?"

"Could be," said Rafferty. "Here's your change."

"That's what I thought," said The Fat Man, taking it. "Wouldn't take much, neither, to jack your earnings up quite a bit. A little sprucing up here and there, maybe a little music to keep things lively—now take me, for instance, I'm a sentimental sort, I like a little music when I drink. Which reminds me," he added, picking up his glass. "Cheers."

"Don't mention it," said Rafferty.

The Fat Man set down his glass. "Good stuff," he

said, smacking his lips, which set his jowls to quivering like custard. "The very best, if I'm not mistaken. Yes sir, a guy like me appreciates the best—and you know, there's a lot more out there like me. Good liquor, good music, and good-looking women—we got a taste for those things. Now take her, for instance"—he jerked a thumb toward Soleful Susie, who had just emerged from the booth at the back—"not bad, not bad at all. But not too good, neither, not the way she's looking at present. Now if you hoisted her skirts up another foot or so, and gave the customers a little something to gawk at . . ." He laughed, and the laugh made him quiver all over. "Well, you get my meaning, don't you?"

"I do indeed," said Rafferty, flashing a glance at Soleful Susie to see how she was taking this. Which to all intents and purposes she wasn't—taking it, I mean. Not that anybody but me could be sure, just by looking; because with Soleful Susie it's sometimes hard to tell.

"Yes, sir," said The Fat Man, "it pays to move with the times. Now this setup here, you got to admit it's kind of old-fashioned." He squinted around. "Not that I'm knocking it, mind you; it's got atmosphere, and that's an asset. But it ain't enough, not by a long shot—not in this day and age. We're living in an age of progress, see; things are changing and they're gonna keep on changing, and we've all of us got to change along with them just in order to keep up. Change is the nature of things, and there's no point holding back from it—it just don't pay, no sir, not in the long run." He leaned forward and waggled his finger at Rafferty. "You know what it is, mister, this Change thing I'm talking about? It's opportunity, that's what it is—and it's the smart guys like me that know how to cash in on it. Yes sir, I got a real nose for opportunity—I can smell it out from a mile off. I never missed a bet, friends tell me; and I daresay they're right about that."

"I daresay," said Rafferty, not batting an eyelid; but I could feel the hackles rising on the back of his neck. Mine would have been rising, too, if I'd happened to have any—which I didn't, not being corporeal just at that moment. That's dangerous talk, you see, the same kind that Barnabas Tobin used in selling his Exopsychic Deontologizer to his backers. *I* should know, seeing as how it was that same talk got me where I am now—not that I'm complaining, mind you, since I only got my just deserts; but all things considered, I can't honestly recommend it, not to those of you who don't have any just deserts coming to you.

The fact was, I sensed a storm brewing. Everything added up to that, now that I stopped to think about it: The Fat Man, the two whiz kids named Fischer and Spassky, and above all the absence of gremlins. It all added up because it *didn't* add up, if you get what I mean. There was no pattern to it that I could see, and that worried me: in a well-run universe like this one there's always a pattern, unless something has gone wrong somewhere.

Maybe I was just imagining things, but I didn't think so. In any case, I figured I'd better check into it, just in case Causality was beginning to get a little out of hand. So I gathered my energies together, concentrating myself, so to speak; and then gave myself a Moebius twist, reversing parity; and all at once I'd slipped over, and was on The Other Side.

I was right about the storm; it was still only in the early stages, building up, but I could tell right away that it was going to be a real humdinger. Even now, when things had hardly got started, it was pretty impressive: great waves of statistical anomaly roaring in to smash and spatter against the frame of Objective

Reality like breakers along a rocky coast; and the gremlins were whooping and hollering and skeering in on the wave crests like California surfers gone berserk with the sheer power of it all. It was a great game for them, no doubt about it; but for me it was different—I didn't dare let myself get carried away. I clung like a limpet to Objective Reality, gluing as much of my attention as I could spare on Rafferty's and its inhabitants and the whole firm, solid, not-quite-unshakable continuum of which they were a part, at the same time keeping a weather eye peeled to take in this storm which was battering at their foundations.

Well, I'm exaggerating a little—actually it wasn't as bad as all that. I mean, the foundations were safe enough, at least in this neighborhood; the chaos threatening us fell somewhere short of being primordial, if that was any consolation. Not like the storm Barnabas Tobin kicked up, when all but one or two of the Eternal Verities were temporarily knocked for a loop and the entire Orderly Frame of Things was teetering on the edge of collapse—this time, I could tell, we were nowhere near the center of the disturbance. Elsewhere, maybe, a galaxy or two would blink out of existence, or a few dozen stars go supernova, or a planet shatter and dissolve; maybe they had already, maybe that was what this tempest was all about. But here on the outskirts nothing much would happen, relatively speaking—things would be shaken up, of course, but no worse than a plague of mischievous gremlins could manage if they set their minds to it; and after a while the forces of Natural Law and Order would slowly but surely reassert themselves. That didn't bother me particularly; the world's survived worse. Maybe it'd even be a good thing, shaking The Fat Man and all the others like him out of their customary self-satisfied complacency—though in most cases, I'm afraid, it'd take more than a mere Probability Storm to manage *that*. Look at what it took to enlighten *me* for instance, and how much it cost me. . . .

But I'm digressing. It's a bad habit of mine—sort of hard to avoid, though, when you're smeared out like I am into a subcorporeal slur of low-order probabilities. But a bad one all the same.

So anyway, there I was, hanging on tight to Reality as if my continued existence depended on it, while all around me waves of Uncertainty beat and shattered. Everything was blurred and kind of hazy, as it always is on The Other Side, and with each wave that came it blurred some more and shimmered out of focus as if it were getting ready to melt and run; and then, as the wave passed, it would kind of waver back again into almost-but-not-quite sharpness, only to shimmer and smear once again as the next wave came. Every now and then a gremlin would come skeering past me, or maybe even through me, and I'd feel it as a sort of electric tingle of joyously untrammeled irresponsibility that didn't have a care in this or any other world. I wouldn't have been human (or ex-human, or whatever you want to call me) if a part of me hadn't leapt at the touch of it and yearned wildly to respond. They were like children at play, all glory and mischief and irrepressible energy rolled up into a tight little frenzy of marvelously uninhibited innocence; and if I was unable to join them in their game I was the poorer for it. But I hung back because I had to—I *couldn't* join in; my sense of responsibility to the Scheme of Things said otherwise.

And besides, I was thinking of Rafferty's and what would soon be happening over there—if it hadn't started already. I wasn't too worried about the rest of the world; all they'd have to contend with was a sudden upsurge of statistical anomalies. Maybe a half a million normally level-headed New Yorkers would all at once take it into their minds to go for a drive through the Lincoln Tunnel, and maybe a couple of hundred thousand bridge players all around the world would pick up their hands and discover they'd been dealt thirteen spades, and maybe all the babies who happened to be conceived on this particular night would be born identical triplets with genius-grade IQ's, and maybe all the cars stacked in all the world's parking meters would be shuffled together so that when their owners paid to retrieve them they'd get back some rather interesting hybrids. Little things like that are none too serious; people take them in their stride, after the initial shock.

But Rafferty's, you see, is a kind of focal point—that's what gives the place its special charm, or a part of it anyway. There are statistical fields just as there are magnetic ones, and they too have poles, and Rafferty's happens to be located smack-dab on top of one of those poles. "The still point of the turning world," old John Edgar Harding calls it sometimes—but only when it's late in the evening and he's getting maudlin. Maybe it's second sight on his part, or maybe it's only the liquor; but anyway, he's right, after a manner of speaking.

So that's why, just then, the Probability Waves were rolling in on me from all directions at once. Don't try to figure out the geometry of it—you can't, because geometry on The Other Side is different from anything you could ever conceive of. You'd have to be crazy to try, like Ludwig Kleinsdorfer was—you know what his formulas did to *him*, and he was nowhere near the truth of it.

But I'm wandering again, which is exactly what I was hanging on trying *not* to do at this time I'm telling you about. Confusion was compounding itself all around me; the last thing in the world I wanted to do was let any of it spill over into myself. Even if old Kleinsdorfer had been there in person, which he wasn't at that particular moment, I'd have done my best to ignore him; I'd have known I was being impolite, him being an old friend of mine, but the last thing I needed just then was a Disturbing Influence, and if there's one thing that can be said of old Kleinsdorfer in spades, it's that he's very much a Disturbing Influence. So instead of him I concentrated on The Fat Man, because I sensed that in some way he was the key to all this, at least in its local manifestations. Either he was a Disturbing Influence himself, a kind of statistical Typhoid Mary, which didn't seem too likely; or else the Scheme of Things was seeking to regain its equilibrium by throwing him in as a counterbalance. If so, God only knew what would happen to him in the end, because the Scheme of Things isn't much concerned about the ultimate fate of its uncomprehending counterbalances, as I know all too well. But anyway, I focused on The Fat Man, and did another Moebius twist, and flipped back over into Our Side.

It was a pretty nauseating experience. I found myself coextensive with The Fat Man, interpenetrating his body so to speak, and I didn't like it. He *felt* as mean as he looked, mean clear through, in every joint and flabby muscle of his body. Sinking into him was like drowning in a pool of warm Jello. But it had to be done, so I gritted my incorporeal teeth and did it.

Something in him felt my presence and resisted. He gave a little twitch, spilling some of the drink he was holding in his hand, and I felt his eyes cross, mean and narrowly calculating. He had stopped talking to Rafferty, somewhere in midsentence, as I slipped into him. Rafferty didn't say anything, but bent to wipe the spilled drink from the counter.

"Jee-zus!" said The Fat Man suddenly. I had an inside view of the fact that he wasn't feeling too good.

At the other end of the bar, old John Edgar Harding turned and looked toward us. "It is you, my good man, is it not?" he said.

"Uh-huh," I said, struggling to control The Fat Man's vocal cords. "It's me, all right—Quintus MacDonald. At your service."

Old John Edgar rose and came strolling over to us. The Fat Man sat rigid, mainly because I was holding him that way—and quite an effort it took, I assure you. John Edgar stopped in front of us. "I gather that there is a Storm brewing," he said deliberately.

"That's right," I said around The Fat Man's greasy tongue. "A big one, coming this way."

"Thank you," John Edgar said. "It is good to be warned." He inclined his head to one side. "You heard, Rafferty?"

"I heard," said Rafferty.

"Perhaps you had best fetch Moira down," said John Edgar. "I have noticed that she frequently exerts a calming influence on such occasions."

"You're right," said Rafferty. He turned and went out through the door behind the bar to call Moira.

"A Storm, you say?" said Louella van Doren from the other end of the bar. She turned to Isherwood Foster. "You've never been here during a Probability Storm, have you, darling? It's really quite thrilling—a once-in-a-lifetime experience."

Isherwood Foster looked as if he hoped to hell it would be.

"You may rely on us," John Edgar assured me. "Even in the moment of crisis we shall not lose our heads."

"Better not," I warned him—with some difficulty, because already I could feel my control over The Fat

Man's body slipping; he was stronger than I'd expected. "Gotta be going—'bye."

"Good-bye," said John Edgar. "And good luck."

I couldn't respond, because I was already engaged in decorporealizing. I exploded out of The Fat Man, and fragments of me spread like ripples to every corner of Rafferty's. For a moment parts of me were simultaneously caught up in the consciousnesses of Soleful Susie, John Edgar Harding, Fischer and Spassky, Byron Wilcox, Isherwood Foster, Louella van Doren, and James Clerk Maxwell, the cat. It was like being jerked in eight different directions at once. Then I caught hold of myself and pulled myself back together. It felt good—you have to have been split eight ways simultaneously to appreciate just how good being a decorporealized microstatistical smear can feel.

Rafferty had just returned, with Moira following him. The Fat Man sat quivering piggishly in front of them. "Something just happened to me, didn't it?" he said in an accusing tone. "Don't deny it—I *felt* it happening to me!"

"Maybe," Rafferty said. "I didn't notice."

"You're lying," said The Fat Man. "I could *feel* it all through me!"

"Don't be foolish," said John Edgar Harding superciliously. "It is nonsense to speak of 'feelings' in reference to a swinish creature like you." He turned and marched back to his stool.

Byron Wilcox stuck his head out from his booth. "Hey, Susie," he wailed, "don't dry up on me! I need another shot."

"Coming," called Soleful Susie. She went behind the bar.

Louella van Doren was explaining loudly to Isherwood Foster just what the last Probability Storm at Rafferty's had been *like*. James Clerk Maxwell was curled up asleep in the rear booth. Undisturbed, the whiz kids Spassky and Fischer continued their game of three-dimensional chess. That's the way things are in Rafferty's: the habitués have learned to take just about anything in their stride.

The Fat Man shuddered. "You could at least call a doctor," he said. "For all you know, I might be dying."

"There's a phone in back," said Rafferty. "You can use it if you want."

"It'll cost you a dime, though," added Moira.

The Fat Man closed his eyes. "*Jee*-zus!" he said again.

At this point something in me tingled, and I became aware that there was a gremlin in the room. Maybe he'd followed me across from The Other Side, or maybe he was one of the regulars who were here most nights—I couldn't say, because I often have difficulty telling one gremlin from another. In any case, I felt a whoop of joy that kind of shimmered in the atmosphere as he spotted The Fat Man. That's torn it, I thought to myself; the trouble's about to start.

The Fat Man shifted on his barstool. Now maybe I'd better tell you that Rafferty's isn't one of those places that have modern-type barstools which are screwed down to the floor; Rafferty insists that his customers prefer the old-fashioned wooden kind that you can tilt backward or forward if you want to. So The Fat Man's stool wasn't fixed down, and there was this little depression in the floor right behind it where it had been worn down over the years; the chances were maybe one in a million that The Fat Man's shifting would slide one leg of the stool into this depression in just such a way that the stool would topple right over—but what's a one-in-a-million chance to a gremlin? I felt the little bugger seize it and give it a sort of a twist; and then it had materialized and The Fat Man was

81

sprawling on the floor, all pink and tumbled like a stranded jellyfish. He'd let out a sort of porcine squeal as he went down, and it seemed to hang in the air and mingle with the silvery tintinnabulation of the gremlin's laughter.

Soleful Susie rushed around the end of the bar and helped him to his feet. The Fat Man sort of leaned on her as he got up; it was like his gross flabby self was oozing around her to swallow her up, just like it had already swallowed up the thin man who was no longer screaming inside. Then he let go of her and leaned panting against the bar. "Jee-*zus!*" he said. "You oughta do something about those goddamn stools—I might of been killed!"

"It ain't the stools," said Rafferty. "It's the gremlins."

"I oughta sue," said The Fat Man. "I'd be within my rights."

"Don't be silly," said Moira. "You can't sue a gremlin."

"An interesting point," said John Edgar Harding from the end of the bar. "Is the proprietor of a respectable establishment such as this one legally responsible for the acts of such gremlins as might be said to haunt it?"

"He isn't," Louella van Doren volunteered. "There was an article about it in *Fortune* just last month. Isn't that right, Ishy darling?"

"That's right," said Isherwood Foster. "I read it myself."

"You see?" said Rafferty to The Fat Man. "Gremlins is classed as an Act of God, so I ain't legally responsible for how they behave."

"That's right, Raffy," said Louella van Doren cheerfully. "I told you this 'ud be fun," she added in a loud aside to Isherwood Foster.

The Fat Man quivered all over with piggy indignation. "What kind of a place *is* this?" he demanded.

"A nice, clean, decent one," said Moira.

"As you can see," added Rafferty.

"Jee-zus *Christ!*" said The Fat Man.

"Here," said Soleful Susie, "if you'll just move aside I'll get your stool set up for you again."

The Fat Man turned and glared at her, like he was contemplating using her for a toilet-plunger, then stumped over to the booth behind Byron Wilcox and eased himself into it. "I could use another drink," he said, obviously doing his best to keep himself under control. "How about it, sister?"

"Be right with you, sir," said Soleful Susie. She upended the stool and set it back in place.

The Fat Man sat glowering. He hadn't left yet, though, in spite of the utmost provocation—which meant that he hadn't just dropped by casually, like he'd tried to make it appear. So he had something on his mind—business, probably; I've had enough experience with businessmen that I can tell. It wasn't good, clean, open-and-aboveboard business, either; otherwise he'd have come right out with it in the first place. I smelled a rat, in other words—a big, pink, slimy one.

I also smelled a couple more gremlins, who'd presumably been whistled up by their friend to come and join in the fun at The Fat Man's expense; they sort of flashed and glittered in the air, like Christmas-tree tinsel. And there was a kind of electric tension building up, as the Probability Storm began to spill over from The Other Side. I felt all taut and tingly and keyed-up; I knew inside that something was about to break.

Two of the gremlins darted over to The Fat Man's booth; I couldn't see what they were doing, but from the way The Fat Man was acting I guessed that they were amusing themselves by triggering off all sorts of itches and twitches and aches in his internal organs. The third gremlin drifted across to the booth where the two whiz kids were sitting; and I drifted over, too, being kind of interested in what might happen to their game. Spassky was bent over the board, about to move a pawn, when the gremlin got to him. He hesitated, then suddenly darted his hand across and shifted his queen one space to the left. Fischer frowned; the move didn't make sense to him. It wouldn't have made sense to me, either, if the gremlin hadn't brushed against me as it left, so I picked up the fact that this particular move would lead inevitably to a mate twenty-three turns later, unless Fischer happened to make exactly the right countermove eleven turns from now. Which he probably would, knowing the way gremlins work; in any case, I was sure this game would be one that would go down in the history books, at least the kind of history books that are read by three-dimensional chess freaks.

Then one of the bottles behind the bar seemed to pick itself up and began to shake itself. It was the molecules of the air doing it—I knew that—and the odds against its happening spontaneously were an uncountable number of trillions to one. There were no gremlins behind the bar—Moira is very strict on keeping them out from there—so I knew it was the anti-statistical chaos from The Other Side beginning to spill over. Isherwood Foster was watching the bottle bug-eyed, while Louella van Doren was prattling along beside him giving a highly inaccurate running commentary on just *exactly* what was happening. The Fat Man in his booth didn't pay any attention; he was lost in his own miseries.

Rafferty picked the bottle from the air and set it down carefully on the shelf. It stayed put. Rafferty has

The Power, so he's quite capable of handling that sort of thing.

Soleful Susie was carrying a couple of drinks across to The Fat Man and Byron Wilcox; suddenly she slipped, and the two glasses flew off her tray as neatly as if they'd been aimed and cascaded their contents down the front of The Fat Man's suit. That was gremlins' work—I could tell. Moira could, too, and she waggled an admonitory finger in their general direction; she doesn't like to have gremlins taking advantage of poor Susie. The Fat Man was too immersed in his internal indignities to pay much attention to what was happening to him.

More bottles started dancing on the shelves, clinking together; the sound gradually formed into the opening bars of Mozart's *Eine Kleine Nachtmusik*. The chance of that happening naturally was infinitesimal. I knew then that the Storm was upon us.

And with it came a flurry of gremlins, tens and hundreds of them. There were so many that from now on I wasn't able to distinguish between what was gremlins' doings and what was caused by the Probability Storm itself. Maybe it didn't make any difference, anyway; after all, old Ludwig Kleinsdorfer has always claimed that gremlins are merely improbabilities personified, much as I am now; and while Kleinsdorfer may be crazy, he isn't so crazy that he isn't absolutely right every now and then. But be that as it may, Rafferty's was chaos from this point on.

For *me* it was pretty chaotic, too, since I couldn't avoid being sucked into it. I corporealized and decorporealized, bunched up and spread out into a spiral wave form, bobbing in and out of various people's consciousnesses, all in a sort of cosmic waltz that whirled me up and dissolved me into dancing almost like a cloud of midges. But my being never quite disintegrated, and I retain all my memories intact—so you can take my word for everything I'm going to tell you. As a matter of fact, I was never the least bit confused—which is quite an accomplishment, and one that I have the right to be proud of.

In the beginning, I've got to admit, I *almost* slipped into confusion. Everything seemed sort of hazy and distorted, as if I were seeing it through waves of flowing water. Everybody except Rafferty and Moira was all out of focus, as if they were on the edge of dissolving into the other people they might have been if their lives had gone otherwise than they actually had. Even the thin man that The Fat Man had swallowed up inside him was back, screaming his head off to be let out—I don't mean screaming out loud, because he had no vocal cords of his own; it was an etheric scream, which only I and the gremlins could hear. Rafferty's flowed too—not the walls themselves, which were solid and secure enough, but the bar and the booths and the stools and all the fixtures, which *might* have been set up subtly otherwise even by a masterhand such as Rafferty's. But all this was only at first; then I began to catch the rhythm and flow with it, and everything became clearer.

But only for a moment. Then suddenly I was bunched up and concentrated inside the consciousness of James Clerk Maxwell. I'd never been corporealized in a cat before; and believe me, it's quite an experience. I was curled up in the rear booth, peacefully dreaming of my happy kittenhood, when all of a sudden it struck me that there were dozens of she-cats I'd known that I might have had but for one reason or another hadn't. The specters of all those might-have-been shes rose *en masse* in my mind as if they were all physically present, a great roiling phalanx of them; the air was redolent with their rich musky scent. That

86

scent was calling me, and I was horny as hell, and I rose and arched my back and yawned and spread out all my front claws, and then I settled back onto my haunches and let out a deep musical yowl that was compounded half of excitement and half of sheer unalloyed frustration at all those golden opportunities that seemed almost palpably present but I knew somehow I'd had the misfortune to miss forever. Then my eyes happened to light on Louella van Doren, who was also emitting a rich musky odor of civet that I could pick up even from here (I suppose it was her perfume; not being gifted with a sense of smell when I'm in my decorporeal state, I hadn't noticed it before); and then all at once, willy-nilly, I was *her* instead of James Clerk Maxwell.

It took me a moment to realize I'd made the shift, because as far as the quality of their minds went, there wasn't too much difference—I'd never realized before how much of a cat Louella is. I spread my claws and clutched them tight on Isherwood Foster's forearm; the poor dear was as rigid as a tight girdle, but that didn't seem to bother me. "Isn't this exciting, darling?" I purred into his ear. And all the while I was tautly aware of the deep masculine musk of him, and of the delectable way his stiff rough whiskers prickled me as I rubbed my cheek against his. I flexed my muscles, and part of me didn't like what was on my mind—the *me* part of me, I mean; after all, I was male once, and I never went in for perversions. But the Louella part of me was positively aglow with excitement, and brimming with a caldron of plans for poor Ishy that fell a long way short of what *I* would consider Creative Marriage Management. "I'm frightened, darling," I whispered, lying through my false teeth. "Hold me close; I'm *scared* what might happen next." And Isherwood Foster held me close, in a kind of death grip. I raked my claws down his forearm. "Oh, *darling*," I said, "you're so *strong!*"

And then, thank God, I was free of Louella and exploding outward. For a moment I was coextensive with the whole of Rafferty's, my consciousness multifaceted as if I had myriad eyes, like an insect. Rafferty, I could see, was breasting the Storm, with Moira at his side; and the two whiz kids, Fischer and Spassky, were completely oblivious to it, immersed in their game. Byron Wilcox had been seized with what he saw fit to term inspiration, and was scribbling down a poem on the napkin that had come with his last drink. The others were more overtly affected. Soleful Susie had collapsed into the arms of old John Edgar Harding, who was stroking her hair and whispering to her something about the Fallacy of the Interminable Asymptote. Louella van Doren and Isherwood Foster . . . well, I already told you something of what was happening there, and I won't go into any further details in case they might embarrass you. The Fat Man in his booth was quivering and twitching like a stuck pig, totally unable to cope with the force of the primal scream that was rising from the thin man trapped inside him. The outlines of the bar and the booths were all blurred, and dancing like a swarm of mayflies above a pond. And through the midst of it all stalked James Clerk Maxwell, his fur bristling, wailing like a banshee for all the loves he had lost and was currently engaged in seeking out again.

There was more, of course, but there's a limit to how much the human mind can assimilate in a single instant—even a deontologized human mind like mine. And I was fast approaching that limit. So with a determined spasm that spread spiraling outward to all the semidissociated parts of me, I pulled myself together. For a moment I found myself concentrated behind the bar, down near Moira's feet. I kind of huddled there, drinking solace and security from the sweet female presence of her. It really *does* mean something to be the seventh daughter of a seventh daughter; it gives one a kind of radiant selfhood that communicates itself like comfort to all those around one. I suppose I'm more or less in love with Moira because of that radiance of hers; I think everybody who's ever met her is, a little, except maybe for The Fat Man. If I was still human I might try to make something of it—I used to have sufficient gall. But then, of course, there's Rafferty, who's not the sort to stand for any nonsense. And anyway, I'm no longer human, at least not in the conventional sense of the word, so there's no point mooning over *that* particular impossibility.

So anyway, there I was, bunched up and feeling all bitter-sweet sad and almost sorry for myself—about not being Rafferty, I mean, so I could have Moira for my very own—and then another wave of anomalies hit me, and all at once I was scattered every which way once again. I scrabbled to collect myself, and all of a sudden found myself half-materialized amongst the bottles behind the bar; but I caught myself in time to keep from knocking them down from the shelf, and managed to waver into somewhat indistinct materiality on top of the bar, directly in front of John Edgar Harding and Soleful Susie.

Susie let out a kind of half-shriek and shrank back, but John Edgar just looked unperturbedly up at me and said: "Well, my good man, you're here in the flesh, I see."

"More or less," I said, panting. "I'll have to be going soon."

"When we must go, we must go," said John Edgar sagely. "That is the way of the world; but we might as well make the best use of the little time available to us.

Let me see, now—the last time we met face to face we were conversing about Barnabas Tobin, were we not?"

"That's right," I said.

"Perhaps we could continue with that conversation," said John Edgar, "for the duration of this brief span that has been vouchsafed to us. The subject is one of professional interest to me, as you doubtless are cognizant."

"I am," I said. But perhaps at this point I should stop a moment and explain that, back in my corporeal existence, I, Quintus MacDonald, was Barnabas Tobin's leading financial backer. That's what got me into the spot I'm in now; and it's also why I'm such an authority on the Exopsychic Deontologizer and its untoward effects.

"Well," I said to John Edgar, "after the Duly Constituted Authorities cracked down, old Barnabas went kind of off his head, as I'm sure you remember."

"I remember it well," said John Edgar, nodding.

"He was convinced people were plotting against him," I said. "Behind his back, as he put it. Which wasn't true; they were being quite open about it, actually. But it didn't make any difference; it just made him feel all the more certain that universal deontologization was the only solution to all the world's problems. So he came to me and begged my support to help him continue his experiments in secret." I shook my head wryly. "And I was fool enough to agree."

"Foolish indeed," said John Edgar. "I would have expected that a person of your acumen would have learned his lesson by that point."

"Well, I hadn't," I said, put on the defensive. "I was merely the twelfth richest man in the world, remember; I'd never developed a head for anything more recondite than making money. And I've got to confess that the idea of deontologization still appealed to me. So it went against the cosmic grain—so what? I was always a contrary-minded sort; it was contrariness that got me where I was then, Lord help me."

"And He did, did He not?" said John Edgar. "He finally demonstrated to you the error of your ways, which was all you ever had any right to ask of Him. But continue, please."

"I'm trying to," I said—a trifle impatiently, because I could already feel the prickling sensation that indicated I was on the edge of dematerializing again. "So anyway, to cut it short, we built another Exopsychic Deontologizer—in secret, of course. It was a small model, distinctly underpowered—it ran on two Eveready dry cells, as I remember—but Barnabas got old Ludwig Kleinsdorfer to check over his calculations, and they both agreed that it would be just barely strong enough to turn the cosmic tide."

"Fascinating," said John Edgar. "Absolutely fascinating. I had never realized that Kleinsdorfer himself was involved . . ." He broke off, perhaps because I was frowning impatiently at him. "But continue."

"So I was there in person," I said, "when Barnabas turned it on. As his backer I'd insisted—the more fool I. It might've worked, too, if we hadn't both of us been overenthusiastic. I insisted that he try it at the top setting—Kleinsdorfer had warned us against that, but we both of us forgot it in the heat of the moment. That was what saved the world, I guess—our overenthusiasm—because the photon tube blew as soon as he threw the switch. So Barnabas and I were the only persons caught in the field during the one brief moment it existed; and of course we were deontologized immediately, and shot straight off to opposite statistical poles, Barnabas off in the Andromeda Galaxy somewhere, and me . . ." I shrugged. "Well, here I am." I was going to say more, but with my shrug a shudder passed

91

through me, and I felt myself starting to disintegrate. I had just time to shout: "Gotta go—'bye for now"—and then I was dematerialized once again, spreading in a wave front that pulsed briefly outward to take in the whole of Rafferty's, the whole continent, the whole world, the whole cosmos.

Infinitely attenuated, I was aware of John Edgar saying: "Farewell, my friend; we must resume our conversation on some more propitious occasion." Simultaneously, I was aware of myriad statistical anomalies taking place throughout the cosmos: a mass outbreak of the screaming meemies in a department store in Newark, New Jersey; a convocation of several hundred laughing hyenas around a half-dry waterhole in Central Africa; a whole rookery of penguins dancing the barcarole in the Falkland Islands; a sudden subsidence of the outermost fringes of Jupiter's Great Red Spot; an indescribably vivid auroral display above the northern hemisphere of the variform planet, Organon; thirty million Casseflavian jub-jubs all sporulating at the identical instant on a world somewhere in the Lesser Magellanic Cloud; further out yet, in an uncharted galaxy well beyond the range of Earth's most powerful telescopes, ten thousand synchronized supernovae spelling out the Velantian ideogram for Mystic Happiness—and countless more, enough so that I could fill a dozen books simply listing them all. Then, with a swirl, I contracted again, and found myself back in Rafferty's.

This time I had locked into the consciousness of Byron Wilcox. He had just completed his poem, and was sitting gazing bemusedly down at it. Along with him I read it over once again:

It happened one frosty look of trees
waving gracefully against the wall:

the cat, the king and I there found surcease
in conscience bound to weary seneschal.
I forget whether he went on and on,
yet go he did; and in the morning spoke
briefly of love and pity—there were none
who mourned for him, and few cared where he
*   woke.*
He said her head shook vertically aligned
in sequences he could not comprehend,
but joy it was to kneel here unconfined
and flex his wings and call his God his friend.
Eve loved intensely all men who must die,
and bowed her hands and closed one weeping eye.

Well, I thought, it rhymes and scans, so it isn't exactly Neo-Dadaist. But I liked it anyway, in spite of the fact that it almost made sense. Briefly I contemplated submitting it to *The New Yorker*, who had been begging for a new Byron Wilcox poem recently; but then I decided against it. This was the kind of verse that could ruin my carefully maintained reputation as the nation's foremost Neo-Dadaist. The critics would unanimously accuse me of deserting The Cause—and they might well be right, at that. Rhyme, meter, and sense—those were the three things that I, Byron Wilcox, had sworn to stand foursquare against. Reluctantly I scrumpled up the napkin on which the poem was written and dropped it onto the floor, where I ground it determinedly beneath my feet.

The other part of me—the *me* part—was trying to calculate the stupendous improbability of Byron Wilcox's ever coming up with a poem that even verged on comprehensibility. But there was no way of figuring the odds against it, so presently I gave up.

And then I was free of Byron Wilcox, and temporarily pretty much in control of myself. The eye of the storm must have just reached us, I figured, so that there was a brief lull going on. I decided to drop over to the whiz kids' booth and see how their game was developing.

It was as I'd expected: Fischer had made the right countermove to Spassky's shift of the queen a dozen or so turns back, and now the game was developing into a very interesting contest that represented a situation which could rise only once in a trillion games between even the most masterly players. Every conceivable move had an indefinite number of potentially interesting game situations branching out from it, and there was no way of telling which player had the advantage. Gremlins apart, I suspected it would lead ultimately to a stalemate; but there was no way to know for sure.

I expanded my consciousness outward, to take in the general situation. For the time being, it seemed, everything had settled down: Rafferty and Moira were ensconced firmly behind the bar, Byron Wilcox was at work on another poem, Soleful Susie had detached herself from John Edgar Harding and got out her compact and was engaged in fixing up her tear-streaked face, Louella van Doren was gently stroking the arm of the still-rigid Isherwood Foster and whispering sweet nothings into his flushing ear, James Clerk Maxwell had given up on his love quest and returned to his booth and was curled up there licking himself, and The Fat Man was collapsed across his table and muttering obscurely to himself something about "Gimpy" and how he should have listened to him while he still had the chance. Even the gremlins were resting, for the moment; but I knew that wouldn't keep up for long.

It didn't. Pretty soon one of them swooped over in the direction of The Fat Man, and the others followed—there must have been a dozen of them or more. They amused themselves by resuming their torment of him. Suddenly he sat back with a yelp and all his buttons popped off, to clatter down on the table in front of him in the shape of a neat exclamation mark. His jacket and shirt bulged open, to reveal a hairless pink expanse of flabby chest underneath. He grabbed at it and started scratching himself furiously, as if he'd just contracted the hives.

Then all the bottles behind the bar started dancing again—this time to the tune of "Waltzing Matilda." The second installment of the Storm was upon us.

I felt everything waver and go hazy, as it had before. Then, before it even had a chance to clarify, a wave picked me up from behind and hurled me straight into the consciousness of Soleful Susie. All at once I found myself decidedly down in the dumps about some bastard named Sam, who'd cut out three years ago and left me in the lurch. I hated Sam; and at the same time, in that particular moment, I couldn't help loving him, because marching across my mind, arm-in-arm with myriad smiling avatars of me, were all the Sams-that-might-have-been, kind, generous, and above all lovingly warm. I realized that I wanted from the bottom of my heart to have Sam back, and to forgive him for everything he had ever done to me. But at the same time I didn't *want* to feel this way, because I knew damn well that the real-life Sam was an unmitigated bastard—and if I needed proof of that, all I had to do was remember all the filthy things he'd done to me before he finally turned tail and ran out. Thinking of Sam brought tears to my eyes, and I reached up and tried to blot them away before they ran and spoiled my makeup. And then old John Edgar Harding was alongside me, and he put his arm around my shoulders and said: "There, there, my dear girl, there's no need to cry; just remember what Plotinus said . . ." And I

95

couldn't care less about Plotinus, whoever in the hell *he* was; but at the same time I was grateful to the old man for at least trying to comfort me—and above all for calling me a "girl," because I knew damn well that I was getting close to the wrong side of forty.

And meanwhile I—the Quintus MacDonald I—was feeling very embarrassed about all this, because I liked Susie and felt somewhat guilty about this forceful sharing of those innermost secrets she never shared with anybody. I struggled to extricate myself before my embarrassment got worse, and finally I succeeded. I flew out of Susie's mind like a cork from a champagne bottle—and fetched up, of course, exactly where I'd least wanted to go, back in the consciousness of The Fat Man.

It was just as slimy as ever, if not more so—like half-coagulated grease in a frying pan. Sinking into it, I could feel the thin man inside screaming at me to let go of him, and I knew a kind of vicious joy in holding him squeezed off. I hated him: he was a pretty decent sort, really, and I hated anything right and decent on principle, because that kind of thing was always standing in my way.

All this was just the general tone of me—by which I mean The Fat Man, from whom I wish to dissociate myself just as far as I possibly can. Unfortunately, that wasn't possible, not at that moment. Like it or not, I *was* The Fat Man, and that meant I was one of the medium-big wheels in something I'm going to call The Syndicate—you know what I mean, and you also know that if you dig too deeply into the subject it's not likely to be good for you. Just look at what happened to Francis Ford O'Donnell and Efrem Z. Weaver . . . but I'm digressing again, aren't I? That's because this particular part of the story is one I don't feel too happy telling; I'd rather not remember it at all. Being inside

The Fat Man isn't the kind of thing you want to write home about: I felt like I was going to be swallowed up in slime at any moment.

But anyway, there I was; and right now I was lost in a kind of gibbering terror, shot through with flashes of memory of a talk I'd had this afternoon with a little squirt called Gimpy. Gimpy, I gathered, had warned me against coming to this place, and like a fool I hadn't paid him any heed. It's haunted, he'd told me; and I'd sat there quivering with laughter at him because he was superstitious enough to believe in ghosts. I didn't believe in them myself, you see; I was an incorrigible skeptic about anything I couldn't buy or latch onto by my own nefarious means. And this *Rafferty's* joint was in a good location—I was mad as hell at Gimpy and my stooges for never even mentioning it before—because if we set up a connection there we could use it to move in on the lucrative trade in grimoires and such with the students at the North American Institute of Parapsychic Technology, who must be ripe for the picking if they were fool enough to fall for the crap peddled in a nuthouse like that. I saw money in it, big money, if it could be handled right. Just get an in with the owner, and pretty soon I'd have him eating out of the palm of my hand—I knew all the tricks; I could do it in my sleep if need be. And here was this meek little milksop of a Gimpy, and he had the nerve to argue with me and say it wasn't worth it, not if it meant going inside that *Rafferty's* joint again; and I sat there laughing and told him that if he was *that* yellow he didn't have to come with me, I was smart enough to look after myself and I'd like to see the ghost that was smart enough to hold *me* back from what promised to be a pretty hot deal.

And now I was scared yellow myself, and wishing to hell that I'd taken Gimpy just a trifle more seriously.

As a matter of fact, I was scared out of my own filthy mind, and right now I was coward enough to admit it. I wanted to get out of here with my skin intact, and once I was out I'd figure some way of getting my own back—I had some boys under me who were pretty slick at arranging that sort of thing. I'd call them in and make arrangements, because nobody and nothing was going to get away with doing things like *this* to me—after all, I had my reputation to uphold. I was mean not just because I enjoyed it, but also because it paid; and I wasn't going to compromise with good business practice just because I was scared as hell right at this moment. No sir, I wasn't the type that compromised—not me.

I'm making all this sound a good deal more orderly and coherent than it actually was, because The Fat Man's mind was pretty confused at this particular moment, and what I picked up from it I picked up in bits and snatches. I fitted it all together later, just about the way I've told it to you (except that I've left out a few of the nastier details; there are some things it's better for your peace of mind not to know); but the way it actually came out, like I said, was sort of in little spurts of lucidity between the terrified gibberings, like this: *Jee*-zus, they're gonna *kill* me if they keep up with this . . . doctor says I gotta watch out for my heart . . . *Jeez*, it felt like it stopped just then . . . should of listened to that goddamn Gimpy . . . if I can only get out of here, I'm gonna call up the Creep—*he'll* know what to do . . . burn the place up, maybe; no, burning's too good for them . . . *owww*, that hurt! . . . gotta get outa here . . . remember what happened to the Don: heart attack, the doc said . . . shows what *he* knows . . . the Creep knows some pretty clever tricks . . . don't leave no traces, neither; nothing for the goddamn cops to latch onto . . . that goddamn bartender:

maybe I could get my hands on that wife of his . . . *Jee*-zus, that hurts! . . . oughta be a law against them ghosts or goblins or whatever they're called . . . they got no right to treat *me* like this! . . . *oooow*, the pain, the pain, the pain . . . Kee-*rist*, I feel like I'm gonna *die* or something . . . gotta get outa here . . . gotta get out . . . get out . . .

Well, you get the general idea. Only I can't find words to make you feel the rancid sliminess of it all, or the cold hard meanness that writhed beneath it—there aren't any words for that; you have to be trapped in the midst of it to know what it's like. As I was just then—drowning in slime, it felt like. And meanwhile the Probability Storm was raging on all around me (every now and then I could feel little side-eddies from it pulsing through me), and anomalies were pyramiding up in incredibly implausible sequences—and there I was, missing all the fun, stuck there inside of The Fat Man and screaming to get out.

I don't know how long it took, because I lost track of time in there. I struggled and struggled, but he seemed determined to suck me down. God, he was strong in his meanness!—toward the end I was beginning to feel desperately afraid that he was even stronger than I was. And then I thought of Moira, and that thought gave me strength. It was as if she were there beside me, fighting along with me. And slowly, with her help, I fought my way up to the surface.

And then, at last, I'd made it and kicked free of him. I can't tell you what a relief that was; it was like something had been suffocating me and finally I was able to breathe again. I flexed myself all over and expanded, spiralwise, almost singing with the sheer joy of being able to move freely once more. For a moment I felt as uninhibitedly loose and carefree as the gremlins must. You have to have been trapped inside a Fat

Man, even if it's only for a few suffocating minutes, in order to appreciate what a joyous thing freedom is.

For a while I was almost dizzy with happiness. And then I began to worry. It wasn't the Storm that was bothering me: that, I could see, was beginning to die down now, and Rafferty's had stood firm, as always. I'd expected it to: Rafferty's is a good, soundly built place—it can weather practically anything. It *has* to be, of course, being located slap-bang on top of a statistical pole—for which fact you should be grateful, if you aren't already, because if it weren't for the solidity of Rafferty's and its regulars a whole lot of anomalies would come spilling out to expend themselves elsewhere, and the local citizenry would find themselves in all kinds of messes that they wouldn't even have thought possible, the very least of which would be having a whole plague of footloose gremlins on their hands. Tear down Rafferty's and all the other places like it, and the world would find itself halfway to being deontologized without the need of a Barnabas Tobin to help the process along.

And *that* was what was worrying me, because I knew what was in The Fat Man's mind, and it didn't bode well for Rafferty's. People like that are dangerous: they don't appreciate what precarious foundations Reality is built on, and they don't realize how easily the whole thing might be toppled if those foundations are undermined. They've been warned often enough, but they stubbornly refuse to believe in the pundits' warnings—which is pretty damn foolish of them, as *I'm* in a position to know. Just think what would happen if the whole world were suddenly deontologized, without any warning—and *you* along with it. Sure, *I've* adjusted to it all right—but how do you think *you'd* react? And even if you could take it, what about your Grandpa Julius and Aunt Maude and all the rest of your family and friends and acquaintances? Half of them would go crazy, at the very least; and what do you think the cosmos would be like if it were half filled with crazy subcorporeal entities, all interpenetrating and intermingling with the sane ones like you and me? It'd make Edgar Allen Schwarzkopf's worst nightmares look like a Shriners' Circus. And that state of things was precisely what The Fat Man and the others of his unbelieving ilk were working to bring on, even though their selfish little souls didn't know it. I shuddered subcorporeally at the very thought.

Something had to be done, and quickly, because I knew that if The Fat Man got out of there and followed through with his schemes, then Rafferty's was in trouble. Fortunately—or maybe it wasn't just fortunate: maybe it was The Scheme of Things using me as an instrument to right its balance—I knew precisely what to do. The trouble was, it depended on enlisting the gremlins to come to my aid.

Now that was a problem, because you can't talk reason to a gremlin. As a matter of fact, there's practically no way of persuading him to go along with anything at all, because there's no way of getting him to hold still and listen. Unless, that is, you have The Power, like Rafferty and Moira; and that was something I'd never been blessed with. The only way I could think of to get the gremlins' co-operation was to start off doing what I had in mind on my own bat, and then hope they'd see it as a new kind of game and join in just for the sheer hell of it.

So I concentrated all my energies and directed them, not toward The Fat Man, but toward the thin man inside him who was screaming to be let out. That thin man was a pretty decent sort actually, as I've already said, and there had to be a finite probability that he might have come into being in The Fat Man's place;

otherwise he wouldn't have been there at all. The trouble was, that probability was mighty low; it was only the event of the Storm that had actualized it at all. And while I had some voluntary control over probabilities, just as the gremlins did, I didn't have very good co-ordination of it, and I knew damn well that I didn't have the ability all on my own to realize something as inherently improbable as the thin man's having grown up in The Fat Man's place. The gremlins could manage it, if I got enough of them in there all pulling together; that was why I needed their help.

So I focused all my attention on the thin man, as I said, and tried my damnedest to imagine what he might be like. It was hard, I can tell you—and not just because, as you may already have gathered, my attention has a tendency to wander at times. It was hard apart from that, hard to imagine The Fat Man being anything other than The Fat Man, all piggish and jowly and mean, let alone to imagine him as slender and dapper and brimming with good-hearted benevolence. But that was the way it had to be.

Slowly a picture of the thin man began to build up in my mind. There was something graceful about him—something catlike and just a little bit effeminate. A delicate smile played on his face, so delicate that you almost had to look twice to be sure it was really there. There was a sort of Old World courtesy about him, and it was easy to picture him helping an old lady across the street or stopping to pat a passing child on the head (somewhat fastidiously) just because he was benevolently taken with its innocent beauty. It was obvious that he would wear a carnation in his buttonhole—a *white* carnation—and probably he'd put on white gloves when he went out for a stroll, and carry a little Charlie Chaplin cane. Yes, I decided, I definitely liked him—he was a little ridiculous, but kind and

amusing. Rather like W. Worthington Enderby, in fact
... but no, I mustn't let my mind wander.

From one corner of my awareness, I noticed that a
couple of gremlins had stopped by to watch what I was
doing. They were definitely curious. I risked a slight
flicker in their direction in order to catch their attention; but they shied away. Disappointed, I went back to
my task. Presently I noticed they were back, and one
or two others with them. I redoubled my efforts.

At last one of the gremlins caught on. The game
amused him, as I'd hoped it would, and I felt him
alongside me pitching in. The image of the thin man
grew clearer in my mind, but I was still all too aware it
was The Fat Man who was in reality sitting in front of
me, grunting to himself and porkily sweating beneath
the strain of my efforts.

But I was lucky: my game was catching on. More of
the gremlins joined in, singly at first and then by twos
and threes, and I felt their whoops of excitement as
they warmed to the task. Presently there were enough
of them at it so that I felt safe to drop out; from now
on they could do a better job without my own unskilled
fumblings to interfere with what they were doing. I
withdrew, distancing myself in order to get a better
view of the proceedings.

At first I could see nothing out of the ordinary, except for a slight golden haze that seemed to cling to
The Fat Man and blur his outlines a little. And then he
started to melt. I mean that literally: great rolls of fat
were oozing down from him and evaporating away into
immaterial ectoplasm. Slowly what remained of him
dissolved into transparency, and within it the
lineaments of the thin man began to waver into form.
Once, briefly, the old Fat Man seemed all at once to
flicker back into being and sit there, flabbily impenetra-
ble—I told you he was strong; and after all he was

fighting for his life, such as it was. His lips were shaping the same words over and over and over, as if they were an incantation by which he hoped to save himself: "I don't believe it . . . I don't believe it . . . I don't believe it . . ." But he'd picked the wrong last refuge to fall back on: unbelieving can never save you, as I think I've already said. It didn't save him, certainly: all at once he blinked entirely out of existence, and the thin man was sitting there in his place. His hands were folded on the table in front of him, and a delicately self-satisfied smile was playing on his lips. I think he saw me, somehow—maybe I'd been concentrating so hard that I was partially materialized there in front of him—because he rose from the booth and picked up his cane and made a courteous little bow in my general direction. Then, after turning to brush the bench off fastidiously, he seated himself again. He was wearing white gloves, just as I'd imagined him, and a white carnation in his buttonhole.

The gremlins dispersed; they'd had their fun. One by one they flickered out; the Storm had died away now, and I guess they figured they'd find more amusement over on The Other Side where the waves wouldn't quite have spent themselves yet. I let my awareness spread outward once more to take in the whole of Rafferty's.

Rafferty himself was standing imperturbably behind the bar, with his arm around Moira. In the rear booth, James Clerk Maxwell was curled up, sound asleep; I took a peek into his mind, and he was dreaming of mice. Across from him, Spassky and Fischer were still immersed in their three-dimensional chess—it was shaping up to a stalemate, just as I'd figured, but the moves they'd been making would give them conversational material for years to come. Byron Wilcox was sitting staring vaguely off into space; I couldn't tell whether he was inspired or simply in a stupor. At the bar, Louella van Doren had her arm around Isherwood Foster; the poor fellow was still as rigid as a post, but Louella didn't seem to mind. Soleful Susie stood dabbing at her eyes—her memories of Sam hadn't quite dissolved away as yet, apparently—while in front of her John Edgar Harding sat hunched forward on the bar, with his chin cradled in his hands. I took a peek at him, and saw that he was mulling over a new insight he'd just had into the nature of the Unrequited Middle.

The thin man leaned out from his booth and waved delicately to Soleful Susie. She nodded at him, shoved her handkerchief back into her sleeve, and went behind the bar to fetch him another drink. Rafferty let go of Moira and set about mixing it. There was a smile on Moira's face as she watched him work—a smile of total devotion. I felt a pang of jealousy shimmer through me, but I held it in.

The thin man got up from his booth and walked gracefully across to the bar. He seated himself on the same stool The Fat Man had occupied earlier. "Nice place you have here," he said to Rafferty. "A very pleasant atmosphere—very pleasant indeed."

"We try to keep things cheerful," said Rafferty, and Moira nodded approvingly.

The thin man looked across at Soleful Susie. He smiled at her and she smiled weakly back. Then he turned to Moira. "An attractive young woman, that," he said to her, loud enough so that Susie could hear. "The two of you add a most agreeable touch to the decor."

"I like to think so," Moira said, smiling. And Soleful Susie flushed with pleasure.

Rafferty turned and set the drink down in front of the thin man.

"That will be a dollar twenty-five, will it not?" said the thin man, reaching for his billfold.

Rafferty waved him off. "Oh, no," he said. "Tonight it ain't necessary. Tonight I got something to celebrate—drinks are on the house."

"On the house?" Louella van Doren said. "Isn't that wonderful, Ishy?" But Isherwood Foster made no reply.

Byron Wilcox overheard, too. He snapped out of his trance and waved enthusiastically at Susie. But Susie's attention was fixed on the thin man, so Moira went to take the order instead.

Old John Edgar Harding raised his head and winked at me. At least, he winked in the general direction of the shelves behind the bar, which was where my major focal node was concentrated just at that moment. I summoned up the energy to half-materalize, and gave him an ectoplasmic wink in return.

Then I decided to fade—I was interested in seeing how things were going over on The Other Side. I refocused myself, gave myself a Moebius twist, and flipped over. I was feeling more cheerful than I had in a long time—maybe I was finally beginning to get over my unrequited passion for Moira—and I wanted to see what the gremlins had come up with for their latest game. Maybe they'd let me join in; I felt like it just then.

And that's the end of this story—at least, it's as good an end as any. All endings are arbitrary, anyway; there aren't any such things in Reality. Everything that *is* stretches on and on and on.

Maybe you don't believe that; but you'll learn eventually. Howard Hopper did, after all; and so did General Wilbur Prescott and Isadora Edison and Lady Beatrice Annabelle Scraggs. Even Edward Everett Peaslake had his intimations, and Ludwig Kleinsdorfer had a theory, as usual. And then there was Barnabas Tobin, of course—*he* learned his lesson in the end; the Scheme of Things saw to that. Just as it saw to The Fat Man, and just as it's seen to me.

Unbelieving can be dangerous, as I told you before. But don't worry about that—Rafferty has a tonic for it.

You'll be around *sometime*, I know. I'm looking forward to seeing you.

Science fiction frequently deals with the tensions between human nature and technological change ... and one of its insights is that people are often more rigid than their machines. Take the phenomenon of a new art form: no matter how marvelous it may seem to us today, we can be sure tomorrow's critics will manage to view its products with a jaundiced eye. So don't be surprised if Robert Chilson's critic of the future sounds remarkably like Pauline Kael or John Simon, for a true critic can't afford to indulge in simple Wonder.

Robert Chilson has published stories in sf magazines for several years, and is the author of the novels **As the Curtain Falls** and **The Shores of Kansas.**

PEOPLE REVIEWS

Robert Chilson

Nothing stimulates the philosophy like a rainy day. On such a day as this, deep-buried thoughts rise to haunt us again. One wonders on such a day, Where have all the people gone? A depressing and melancholy thought on a melancholy and depressing day.

Despite our vaunted technology, of all the miracles of the weatherconditioners, still a day of rainy-gray arouses such reflections. And not only the failures (or successes) of modern technology. The state of the recording industry alone would imbue with melancholy and depression the sunniest, rarest day in June. We seem to be living in the last days of the life recording.

(It's a rainy day and this month's selections are rainy-gray. But how long has it been since *you* absorbed a great life?)

The first item this month is from Avongarde and is intended for the dishwater religious element: *One Nun's Life*. Even without the admiring quotations from cardinals and archbishops, Sister Angela's life recording provides all the proof anyone needs that the religious establishment is dead, totally and irrevocably. Sister Angela has spent twenty years praying and contemplating the Eternal ache in her knees, and can only conclude that Heaven must be like this. The watery piety of the life—actually it's an exercise in self-flagellation, not religion—is its distinguishing flavor. The whole twenty years of nunnery life blend together in a gray perspective in which time seems not to pass. This is evidently partly the fault of the publisher, who is noted for cutting recordings too short. But Sister Angela's own cuttings, necessary as they are to compress twenty years into two hours, are not convincing. We get the feeling that she has the same impatient thoughts and brief angers we all have, but has cut them out.

For contrast, consider Cardinal Soubert, a deeply religious man with a finer understanding of the human mind. His life record consisted primarily of just these slips and lapses from his ideal, and of his repentances for them; we had a memorable and moving record of one man's search for perfection. It is still a classic. Sister Angela's clumsy attempt to demonstrate perfection will be forgotten by tomorrow night.

It's things like these that tend to shake our faith in the modern world—those of us who have any left on reaching maturity. Our artificial modern life simply does not produce the great lives of thirty to fifty years ago. The techniques of life recording have improved until anyone can play. We are flooded with them now. Yet, where are the great recordings? How often do we have to observe that it isn't the recording, excellent though the techniques may be, but the life, that must be great? To make a great recording one must live a great life. It's as simple as that.

The "Sister Angela" syndrome is very common these days; indeed, it dominates the recording industry. It may be defined as a deliberate attempt to produce a great recording by duplicating the outward circumstances of life of those who recorded classics in the past. In this instance it is Wayne Hoyt Chen who is being copied, by Alberto Helding (*All God's Seasons,* RCA). Chen was a *natural,* a man who had always lived on the land, had never thought of living elsewhere, and was not well-enough educated to confuse himself with Thoreau. Mr. Helding, by contrast, is a modern man, articulate, well-educated, and possessing the romantic modern attitude toward the soil and the life thereon. Herein lies the falseness of this work of life, a paradigm of the falseness of modern life.

Chen's recording makes plain to us the true attitudes of the sons of the soil: pragmatic, unromantic, yet with an underlying feel that the land has always been here and always will be. We who live so far from these our roots cannot share this latter conviction (particularly in view of current trends and the world situation). When one of our kind, as, say, Mr. Helding, attempts to bring his erudition to bear on the land, the result is either a painful disillusionment or a slickly shallow rationalization.

Let me be specific. I recall particularly an episode in Wayne Hoyt Chen's *My Land and Me,* a mere vignette at end of day. Chen had finished his barn chores and paused by the pumphouse to watch the sunset. I was conscious of a deep but not unpleasant ache in my leg muscles and back, and a feeling of pleasant lassitude. Chen's work-hardened muscles did not ache easily, so it must have been a hard day's work. But his thoughts were of pleasure, satisfaction, that so much had been achieved, that this day had not been wasted, that the sunset was so beautiful. Even so, he thought fleetingly of checking the meters to see if his sunpower panels had replaced the power he'd pulled in the day's work.

By contrast, Mr. Helding ends a day feeling a throbbing ache in every limb and muscle (even his eyeballs throb), thinking of his aches and how necessary and, somehow, important they are. "It's always like this; if you want anything, you must work for it," he thinks consciously and clearly, clearly aware of the recording headset. This is a piece of bucolic philosophy much in favor in liberal circles thirty years ago and not wholly displaced even now, a part of the egregious back-to-the-land movement that was, if possible, more artificial than the cities that gave it birth.

Most of the back-to-the-landers dropped out when they found how much and what kind of work it entailed. Mr. Helding has not spent enough time on the land to achieve this disillusionment, or to begin to acquire the deeper wisdom that lies below it. Be it noted that Wayne Hoyt Chen never philosophized. His *attitude*, shaped by a lifetime subject to the vagaries of the weather, of the universe he saw around him, was profoundly philosophic. But he was not, and true naturals are not, articulate. Their thoughts lie deep and rise slowly, not the facile flashes of wit that pass for wisdom in our shiny-surfaced circles.

This is of a piece with the whole "philosophy" of this false life: it is book philosophy, learned beforehand, the "life" merely lived to confirm it—like Sister Angela's religion. On one occasion Mr. Helding sits down (feeling no aches or pains) and proceeds to ruminate about life and how to live it. This was done in a carefully chosen woody setting, and Mr. Helding, a natural teacher, seizes on every bird and squirrel to give his laborious thoughts an air of spontaneity. I say an *air* of spontaneity, for I am convinced that Mr. Helding sat down at his desk previous to this touching scene and outlined his thoughts on a typer, checking the best references and carefully memorizing his points in order. The whole soliloquy is patterned on Thoreau's ruminations in *Walden,* particularly the conclusion, and Mr. Helding is at pains to contradict him to demonstrate his own independence. Throughout the performance—no other word will do—one is conscious of Mr. Helding steering his thoughts away from something taboo—no doubt his notes. One wonders how many takes were necessary.

For an art form that promised us genuine spontaneity, untainted by artistic considerations, however, the perversions of a Helding are small potatoes. *Happening '37!* (Columbia) is a lesson in forced spontaneity. The whole operation has the classic format: get together a group of glittery names, throw them into a party replete with novel sensations, and record their reactions. Should be good for a few million sales. . . . In our view, it isn't good for anything.

This is the debasement of a great artistic medium to the production of cheap thrills, and those who lend themselves to it are prostitutes, glittering names or no. The whole shoddy performance (yes, the performance is as shoddy as the concept; the actors arrived braced and stimulated—and drugged—to be spontaneous) reminds us of a comment of Willis Lehman on an early erotic recording of an old hooker's memories of her greatest tricks: "There is something vague and hazy about these memories. One does not doubt that the tricks were taken. One senses, however, that the memories are more thrilling."

Down among the rukh of "My Operations" and "My First Babys" and "How I Lost Mine," one finds occasionally a small gem. *The Moon Also Rises* (Avongarde) is the deeply moving record of one father's struggle to win his five-year-old daughter's love over the affection of the professional parents with whom she was placed at birth. This is a triumph, not for "natural" parentage, but for love *qua* love. Perhaps most moving is the young man's realization of the harm his love might do to his daughter (he is eighteen); since he had literally no one else in the world, he would tend to dominate her interests in an unhealthy manner. But in the end he has won over even the proparents, who now permit him to visit daily. Such small triumphs strengthen us all.

"What we feel, we know." But do we? I am reminded of the thriller in which a professional water-skier was driven mad by being forced to absorb, over and over, a recording of a tyro's first attempt at water-skiing. Some few years ago there was a fad for lovable failures, born losers in the throes of humiliation. Hundreds of undistinguished young men and women wore recorders on dates, while teaching their first classes, etc., clearly hoping to produce a comic masterpiece. They merely contributed to the "rukh" mentioned above. We learned nothing important about them as individuals or ourselves as a mass; and the life recording after all was trumpeted as the greatest humanizing force in history, the "art of arts."

In retrospect it's easy to see that famous golfers' recordings of how they won tournaments would teach the average duffer nothing—unless he was of precisely the height and weight of the recorder, with the same length of arms, etc. Much the same is true of any other

113

physical education. Granted, in some areas—swimming, for instance—true learning is possible, the life recording can impress the proper responses upon the scanner's synapses. But of how much use is such physical culture in the modern world? Knowledge is what we need, and that cannot be implanted by life recordings. Any knowledge implanted deliberately simply remains there in an unconsulted heap of facts—brickbats, as Mark Twain would say. Knowledge absorbed as a part of another's life is not integrated as a whole into the scanner's personality; only bits and pieces of it are. Obviously, except in rare cases, the individual's personality dominates (though affected by what he absorbs).

Thus it would seem that the only way in which life recordings could be of aid in education is in studies of creativity, in letting the student experience the methodical putting together of parts, the surging unhappy feeling of something undone, forgotten, left out, the illumination of the final "inspiration," and the sheer joy, looking back, of what one has done. But. Although creativity is a learned activity, one that can be and is taught, it cannot be taught by recording. The scanner is too passive, he does none of the work. This too should have been obvious in advance. Nor does it, it seems to me, teach us much *about* creativity, which for all our recordings of this strange phenomenon, remains as mysterious as ever.

This "Queen of Arts," this great humanizing force, is restricted, then, to teaching us how it feels to be "The Other Guy." This is certainly a great force, and can be and has been used to teach us much we only suspected about ourselves before. But even here the most popular recordings are the most superficial, erotic recordings being the most popular. These teach us much about the shape and size and texture of each others' bodies, but nothing of each others' minds.

There is a further hurdle. When one puts on a recording headset, one feels an immediate compulsion to *feel* something—something amplified. What do you say into a microphone? This contributes a sense of strain, often noted. Also, we do not spend our time wallowing in emotion; a rather dull or weary emotion is common to most people most of the time. But recordings consist of the peaks; the dull areas are cut because they slow the action, they take time, and they do not affect the development of the recording personality in any case.

Thus we have a whole generation of people who believe that they are not really alive unless they are continuously at peak (or under a life playback). The milder, human emotions get cut along with the dull ones. Who notices a recording of the guy next door, the guy whose life is as dull as ours? Ah, but his thoughts? his moods? his emotions? *This* is the life we should be learning from life recordings, the *inner* life that is the most truly human thing about us.

There can be no question about it. Life recordings must return to this human channel if they are to survive as an art form. This month's most interesting recording is a collection of minor pieces, "essays" he calls them, of the great critic and man-of-men, Willis Lehman. *Me, Myself, and I* (Columbia) exemplified just the cultivation of the inner life mentioned above, and for all the unimportance of these fragments of Mr. Lehman's fleece, they are far more interesting and informative than anything else we have seen this month. Here is a fascinating piece from the early days of life recordings and of Mr. Lehman's youth. In it Mr. Lehman simply reads the scene in *Henry IV* where Ancient Pistol keeps slapping his hilt and roaring,

"Have we not Hiren here?" and Doll Tearsheet and Mistress Quickly are half fainting. Shakespeare does not tell us what Falstaff's mood or expression is throughout this scene, and we are fascinated by the young Mr. Lehman's mental glimpses of the old man's contemptuous amusement at Pistol's antics and the women's fear, of his sudden rage and the shrewd calculation with which he realizes that kicking Pistol out will endear him, Falstaff, to the women. Of course Falstaff is now known not to have been the cowardly blatherskite he was generally believed to be in the twentieth century.

Here, too, is Mr. Lehman's attempt to cook a meal of wild plants according to the instructions in H. Morgan Morgan's life recording, the horrible mess he makes of it, and—in the humiliation comedy school of life recordings this possibility is never considered—here is Mr. Lehman's analytical approach to his mistakes and the brilliant improvisations by which he extracts himself to produce a tolerable meal. For sheer joy-of-life and the gusto of living, this "essay" alone is worth the price of the recording.

The bulk of the life recording is Mr. Lehman's reactions to famous life recordings he has absorbed and on which he has written: *recorded while he was absorbing them,* a technique new to us and one that opens whole worlds of ghastly recordings. Will a recording of someone's reaction to Mr. Lehman's reactions to these recordings be marketed next? —Despite these forebodings, the trick is a huge success, again because of that warm and human inner life of Mr. Lehman, which shines through his reviews and makes him more interesting than the people he reviews. Here is his reaction to such classics as *The Destruction of New Orleans, Death of a Saint,* and Dr. Koenig's close passage of the Sun, *A Descent into Hell.*

Mr. Lehman's reactions here suggest to us the failure of the younger generation in the recording of lives. So few of them are educated except via the haphazard manner produced by absorption of many recordings that they have no strong skeleton of knowledge to compare with what they learn, either firsthand or through recordings. Indeed, since opinions rather than facts are most easily implanted, *opinions* learned under the playback may prevent their accepting *facts* learned at first hand. Further, since they have commonly begun absorbing lives, even adult ones, at age seven and eight, their development has been fragmented; they are merely walking, ill-integrated heaps of castoff bits and pieces of other and stronger personalities. Such people are capable of nothing original, not even emotions. They have no life of their own.

But Mr. Lehman's own strong, unique personality is evident at every moment, even amid the destruction of a great city, even among the outreaching flames of "Hell," not merely his emotions but his intellect. We feel him observing, wondering, wishing the recorder would turn his head a little to take in a detail; we feel his immediate critical reaction to any false note, any studied effect, any stereotyped or clumsy emotion. He is never lost in the welter or flow of emotion, and when he lifts the playback he suffers no confusion of identity.

One minor piece is I think a perfect example of the sort of spontaneity we expect whenever we plug in a new recording, as well as of that inner life mentioned above: his hearing of Mather's Second Symphony. At first he is attentive to the music, with which he is not very familiar, then his mind wanders to the life of Mather (with whom he was acquainted), then to music in general; is recalled to the symphony by a sudden flourish; wanders again over heroic music, then into the problem of creativity, and from there to the problem of genius, and twenty minutes later awakes with a start when the record clicks off, having heard only the opening. Note especially his wry reaction to his weakness.

Now this by God is *life* recording as it should be, and if anyone, by what prodigies of cutting and splicing don't matter, succeeds in producing a full two-hour, many-year record like this, it will be a classic that will outlive this century—yes, and many others to come. It's all here: the strong, fascinating mind, his thoughts, interesting in themselves, his feelings about the things he thinks about, his sudden realization of how he has lost control of his thoughts, and the wry realization of humanity at the end. There are no "peaks" here, but who could wish or hope to be more alive than this man at this time?

The record closes with Mr. Lehman's reactions to Theodore Wertham's review of Lehman's famous book of life-recording reviews, *In Search of Life,* recorded as he read the review the first time. All that has been said about this recording, *Me, Myself, and I,* can now be repeated about this one final essay. It is Mr. Lehman at his warmest, most delightful best.

—Inner life. Spontaneity. Rain, gloom, and chill. Is it not a portent that the best recording of the month is a mere unrelated collection of bits and pieces from a man of eighty? Where is the vivacity, the joy, the gusto, in any younger person? Where is the *life* they seek to record?

The multibillion-dollar life-recording industry is in no danger; it will continue to show a profit and will outlive this century. But the art! The art!

"What is reality?" is a question that's been explored frequently in science fantasy, but somehow it has remained for George Alec Effinger, in this eerily quiet story, to suggest its logical reply: "Does it matter?"

George Alec Effinger's science fiction books include the novels **What Entropy Means to Me** and **Relatives,** and a short story collection, **Irrational Numbers.**

Ibid.

George Alec Effinger

Cathy Schumacher dismissed the nine o'clock class and gathered up her notes. It had stopped raining during her lecture, and she was thankful. The air outside was chilly and damp, and the Old Quad was an ugly marsh, stripped by the March rains of all the charm that often lured the freshmen to the university. Her stylish boots were providing a minimum of protection, and by the time she had crossed to Krummer Hall she was in a foul mood.

She hated being caught in the jostling crowds of students, on the way from one class to another. She did not hurry across the Old Quad, despite the weather. When she got to Krummer it was already a quarter past ten; everyone else was in class, and the narrow, dim halls were empty. She went to the English Department offices to get her mail. Of course, there was nothing of any interest: a couple of advertising letters from publishers, selling textbooks to any and all instructors, whether they were in the right department or not; two papers from her sophomore seminar, both overdue by two weeks; a notice from the Department Head concerning the locking of offices after five P.M.; a notice from a radical student organization; an exhortation to give blood; a copy of the *Journal of the Institute for Early English Studies.* Cathy took this bundle of paper and went to her little cubicle.

According to her schedule she was required to be in her office in Krummer from ten until noon. Cathy wanted nothing more than to go home and go back to bed, and nothing less than to listen to disappointed pupils chiseling points on an old exam. But her office hours were essential to the educational process; she knew that someday, perhaps, a real student might want to see her. She often wondered if there might not be a genuine serious young man or woman in one of her classes, hiding in the back of the room, burning with a love for Anglo-Saxon poetry. The idea was too absurd, and Cathy dismissed it with a skeptical laugh.

She put on the light in her office, tossed the mail on her desk, hung up her coat, and sighed. She went to the window, which looked out from the back of Krummer, onto College Street and the old city common of New Aulis. It was difficult to picture Ivy University in the old days, the days of straw boaters and football legends. Teaching in the university, she was forever surrounded by its heritage, never far from paintings and statues from its snobbish past. But now College Street was lined with parking meters and litter baskets, and the city common sheltered drunks and dropouts, just as in any other city. The proud statue of the Ivy Patriot that guarded the Main Gate was used by the early-arriving undergraduates as a hitching-post for bicycles. Cathy sighed again; whenever she got her feet wet she began questioning her profession.

The top of her desk was well hidden. Cathy sat down and shoved some of the books from the middle. She scooped up a handful of pens and markers and put them into an ugly white mug. The mug had a picture of the Taft Hotel on it, with the words *Greetings from New Aulis!* beneath it in gold script. Letters from department officials and university officers stuck out among the books, typed on university stationery, with the bright-blue seal catching her eye again and again. Cathy arranged the day's mail in the little cleared space. She thought about sweeping the rest of the stuff to the floor, but she picked up one of the tardy papers instead and tried to concentrate.

She read three pages and stopped. The paper was about "The Battle of Maldon," written in a marginally literate manner. No paragraph in the paper had any ideas in common with any other. The small informational content was stolen either from Cathy's own lectures or boldly from the textbook. Ragged, thoughtless style and typographical errors had long ago ceased to amuse her, and this morning Cathy just didn't have the courage to finish reading. She put the paper down and tried the other. It seemed worse. It was Tuesday; the owners of the papers surely wouldn't ask about them after class on Thursday. After all, they were the ones who had submitted them late. Cathy had a good week to grade them. She certainly wasn't in any hurry now.

The advertising letters, the notice from the Department Chairman, the student organization broadside, and the blood bulletin she crumpled together and threw into the wastebasket. "How quickly I could clean this desk," she thought, "if only the wastebasket were larger." That left only the Journal. It might afford some amusement, at least until the first pupil knocked on her door. Cathy opened the magazine, to see who was publishing and who was perishing.

At ten twenty-five the Sueza Tower carillon played a familiar theme from Dvorak's Ninth Symphony. Cathy had read the "Letters to the Editor." By ten forty-five she had finished an article by one of her former professors at Delta University. The bells were exercising on a scrap of *Parsifal*. Still no one had interrupted her. Cathy pushed her chair further from the desk and slouched down, searching for a comfortable position. She paged through the rest of the magazine, finding the "About People" and "News and Views" pages and looking for familiar names. The bells stopped their serenade, and for several seconds there was silence. Cathy looked up, a bit uncomfortably; the tower chimes struck the hour. She began an article that, for the millionth time, attempted to compare the kennings of *Beowulf* with Homeric metaphor. She read rapidly, absorbed in the article. The message was minimal, but the beauty of the quoted kennings, and the lesser, badly translated phrases of Homer, carried her through the tedious academic exposition. Abruptly, too quickly for her pleasure, she came to the last line of the essay:

—*many times before. The beauty of the work will never tarnish.*[17]

In a habitual motion, Cathy glanced down at the bottom of the page to check the footnote. It read:

[17]*Hello, Mrs. Cathy Schumacher!*

Cathy stared at it for a moment, feeling an unpleasant surprise. She turned back to the first page of the article. No, the author's name was completely unfamiliar, some associate professor who had gone to Southwestern Utah State and was now teaching at Culpden College. Who could it be? Certainly the Journal wasn't the sort of periodical that would permit that kind of horseplay. None of the other notes in the piece had been out of the ordinary. Cathy looked through the rest of the magazine, but the contents were as staid and dry as usual.

The tower chimes struck the quarter hour. Cathy stood and looked out the window. It was drizzling again; people were running along College Street, ducking into doorways to get out of the cold rain. It was darker now. The sounds from the street seemed louder to her, they seemed to intrude aggressively on her attention. While she stared through the window she felt herself becoming sick, with a tightness in her stomach that might never again go away. Cathy forced herself to turn away, to look at the Journal still resting on the desk. She picked it up and walked out of her office.

Her small cubicle was only one in a series along a hallway in the English Department. Two offices down was Wally Chance, an instructor with a Milton course, a Chaucer course, and a freshman survey course. Wally was a good friend, one of the few Cathy had within the university. Though his door was closed, light shone through the frosted-glass panel. She knocked, and he called permission to enter.

"Hi, Wally, it's just me," she said, taking the chair by his desk.

"Hello, Cathy. I was just going through these freshman papers. Thanks for coming by. Another couple of pages and I might have done something evil."

Cathy laughed. "What we have to do is find some other thing for the kids to do. Lord, I get tired reading those papers."

"Just being tired I could handle," said Wally, throwing the paper he was reading back on the pile. "I don't know. I get so angry sometimes. How is it that every one of them can read a book and not even know what they're reading? I mean, somehow they've each managed to avoid realizing that *Pride and Prejudice* is a funny book."

"Where grades are concerned, there's nothing funny."

"Well," said Wally, "that's a shame, then. It makes my job harder. I can't imagine how it must be in their place."

"You were there once, remember?"

Wally looked up and smiled. "Yes, maybe, but I was unconscious most of the time."

"You stay that way until graduation. It's a defense mechanism."

Wally stood and came around his desk. "You want to see a real first-class defense mechanism?" he asked. He took her arm and led her to the door. "Come on, let's go eat."

"I've got another thirty minutes of office hours left," she said, not really protesting, mentioning the fact out of a slight responsibility to form.

"No, don't worry," said Wally. "The kids don't come to see you until after midterms. Anyway, you came here to see me, right? Any reason?"

Cathy went through the door, followed by Wally. She watched him lock his office. She took a deep breath. "Yes," she said, "sort of. Nothing important, though." They walked back to her office to fetch her coat.

"Fine," said Wally. "Lunch-type conversation. If we were going to talk about something important, we ought to stay here in your luxuriously appointed headquarters. For the official atmosphere."

"No, Wally, just let me lock up." She picked up the Journal, with one finger marking the page that had so unaccountably frightened her. She took her coat from the hook and flicked off the lights. As a sudden afterthought, she put the Journal back on her desk. She would feel foolish carrying it all around the campus with her; surely no one else would see the disturbing side of the incident. Wally would tell her that it was funny, and flattering, and a surprisingly free thing for the Journal's editors to allow. She didn't want to see the article. She didn't want to think about the greeting, or where it had come from.

They went to lunch at one of New Aulis' more popular hamburger-and-french-fry counters, rather than one of the university's dining rooms. Cathy explained that she really wanted to get away from the school for a little while. It didn't matter that the hamburger place was filled completely and only with university students, some of whom she recognized from her classes. She was grateful just to sit at the noisy counter, concentrate on the cheap food, and forget everything that had to do with her job. At least, that was what she consciously wanted; somewhere deeper in her mind, something wouldn't let her get away that easily.

Halfway through the lunch, Cathy looked at Wally and said, "Do you ever have things happen to you that you can't explain, even when you know that there has to be a good explanation?"

"What?" said Wally, his mouth full of food, his expression a little startled.

"You know," said Cathy, uncomfortable now that she had begun the subject. "Something strange will happen, and you'll look at it and say, 'Okay, it may look odd, but here are the reasons.' But the reasons just don't satisfy you on an emotional level."

"All the time. I've got three kids, remember?"

"No, no," said Cathy, a little annoyed. "Intellectually I can accept it fine. Emotionally, though, I don't know what to feel."

"I'll bite," said Wally, sighing. "What happened?"

Cathy hesitated. "I shouldn't even have brought the whole thing up. I mean, if I tell you exactly what happened, it will sound awfully trivial to you. But it isn't trivial to me. That's what I mean. Just forget it."

"Nothing easier," said Wally, smiling. "But if I can do anything . . ."

"It's not desperate or anything," said Cathy. "At least there's that. I'm not forced into any kind of action. I just don't know what to think about it."

"You know, I'm not even curious. Someday, though, why don't you lay the whole thing out for me. After you've figured out the meanings, though. I've never been very good at deduction. My experience with my kids proves that. I can never tell when they're lying. My wife can, she can spot it in a minute. All I can do is spot when their reasoning is fallacious. That comes from grading too many papers. I think I've lost a valuable defense mechanism."

"Then so have I," said Cathy. They paid the check, got up, and went to the door. From there, Wally was going back to his office, but Cathy had decided to go home. "I shouldn't let little things like this bother me," she said, "but right now that's all there is in my life. Little things. Mostly like you said, grading papers, listening to stupid kids begging for grades. And going home to hear about Victor's hard day at the microfilm and Leslie's hard day at elementary school."

"It's really true," said Wally. "It's true, really true. I'm not mystified." He smiled and pressed Cathy's hand. Then he turned and started to walk back toward the campus. Cathy went in the opposite direction, toward her small apartment.

It would be a few hours before Victor came home, and still quite a while before Leslie banged through the front door. Cathy dropped off her coat on the kitchen table, checked the refrigerator and the bathroom to see what she had to get at the supermarket, picked up her purse, made certain that she had her keys and money, and went back out. The rain had stopped, but the sky was still an ashen-gray color. All the way to the supermarket, she wondered if it would be worth the effort to call the editorial offices of the *Journal of the Institute for Early English Studies*. Maybe someone there could explain the footnote to her. She shook her head. The whole thing *was* stupid, in a way, and the only problem seemed to be the superfluous emotional importance she was attaching to it. She shook her head once more, to clear it of those thoughts, and tried to think about shopping. She succeeded only partially.

She had to wait by a checkout counter for a grocery cart. The store was crowded and noisy; in a way, Cathy was grateful. She could give her full attention to the petty annoyances of people idly clogging up the aisles of the supermarket. When she got a cart, she steered it along the far wall, making a quick inspection of produce. Victor wouldn't eat any vegetables but corn and green beans. Leslie would okay the corn, but she wouldn't eat the green beans. The Schumacher household ate a lot of corn. Cathy spent an irritating half hour roaming up and down the aisles, trying to plan a dinner, trying to avoid the other people in the store, all of whom seemed not to know what they were doing. At the checkout counter, while waiting for the cashier to total the purchases of the woman ahead of Cathy in line, Cathy started to read a magazine from the small display rack. She turned idly through the pages of a movie fan magazine. How different it was from the things she usually read! The content, the style, the whole attitude . . .

Cathy realized what she was doing and stopped herself abruptly. It was pure intellectual snobbery to try to criticize the fan magazine on the same grounds as she evaluated her colleagues' articles. It was also a very unattractive trait, one she despised in other people. She

127

began to read an article titled "Jamison Hawke—His Fear of Animals." Cathy knew from Leslie's recitations of movie matinees that Jamison Hawke starred in a series of inexpensively produced movies about Gror, the Wild Man. The first sentence in the article made her catch her breath. It said:

Cathy Schumacher, you have to listen! It's important!

She stared at the magazine page for a while, until she numbly realized that the checkout girl was totaling Cathy's purchases, many of which were still in the shopping cart. Cathy finished unloading the cart, and added the movie magazine. She felt lightheaded and dizzy, she felt panicked, and she didn't know why. All she wanted was to understand. That didn't seem like such an unreasonable request. The checkout girl told her how much the bill came to; Cathy took the money from her purse and paid it, then carried the bag of groceries out of the supermarket and back to the apartment. The movie magazine was sitting on top; Cathy didn't look at it the whole way home.

After Cathy opened the front door to her apartment, she carried the bag of groceries into the kitchen. She pretended she was just going to put everything away, just like always, just like normal. She started humming, all the while knowing that she was being absurd, that there was no one else to fool except herself, and she wasn't doing a very good job of that. She put the magazine face down on a counter and sorted out the rest of the groceries. When they had all been put away and the bag folded and stored beneath the kitchen sink, Cathy picked up the movie magazine and carried it into the living room. She sat down on her chair and began riffling idly through the pages of the magazine. At once she saw the Jamison Hawke article, and she saw the message directed to her. Not even in a footnote this time . . . How many thousands of other readers will wonder what it means . . .

As a sudden inspiration, Cathy looked at the front of the magazine; it had been copyrighted two months earlier. She had forgotten that there is such a time lag between when a magazine is put together and the time it's purchased. The footnote in the Journal had shaken her badly. Nevertheless, she could pass that off as a kind of joke by some unknown friend or associate. But who would ever guess that she would even glance through such a magazine as the movie fan thing? No one could have planned that.

She took another glance at the article and the message to her. It made her feel terrible, in a way she felt only in her worst dreams. She could understand the feeling well enough: a sense of being lost in otherwise familiar surroundings; the knowledge that someone was doing something that concerned her, but she was powerless to understand what those plans were. She felt abandoned, and she knew that logically analyzing the situation didn't make it any easier to accept. She had never gone along with the Freudians; just because she could perceive the roots of her neuroses, that didn't imply that they would then disappear. They never had in the past; and now she couldn't perceive anything. Nothing but the two anonymous messages.

The second one had been a kind of a warning, hadn't it? In that case, what should she do? She sat for a moment, feeling her stomach tighten and her hands begin to tingle. The answer was obvious. There wasn't anything to do. Not until she knew what was happening.

Leslie wouldn't be home for at least another hour and a half. Cathy walked around the apartment, aimlessly picking up bits of clothing, putting books back on shelves. She stopped herself suddenly, realizing she was genuinely frightened. She wanted to be out of the apartment, but she couldn't think of anywhere else to go, except back to her office, and that was where the whole situation had begun. That thought gave her an idea, and she went to the phone. She dialed Wally's extension, and she listened to the phone ring for a long time, until one of the English Department secretaries answered and said that Wally had left just a little while before. Cathy couldn't bring herself to call him at home. She was still afraid he'd think the matter was foolish; she doubted that she could convince him of the fear it was generating in her.

Cathy put on the television and tried to absorb herself in the afternoon programing. She found that very difficult. One alternative would be to read through a couple of professional journals and popular magazines that had built themselves up into a large stack on the coffee table. She picked up the topmost magazine, a two-week-old copy of *Time*. On the cover was a picture of someone's advisor for something. He was looking happy. Cathy wondered if he ever had to worry about how his name might turn up in magazine articles. She started to read the issue, but then she began to feel panicky again, and put the magazine back on the pile. She didn't want to make any more discoveries in one day. The nervousness didn't go away; she got up, went into the bathroom, and took a couple of small blue tranquilizers. In fifteen minutes, she was relaxed and unworried again. She watched the end of a give-away show, then a panel quiz program, and then a rerun of a situation comedy that was at least eight years old. Leslie came in, slammed the door behind her, and stalked to her room without a word. Cathy shrugged. In an hour Victor would be home, and things would all be back to normal.

It was getting near dinnertime. Cathy sighed loudly,

dumped the newspaper TV section from her lap to the floor, and went into the kitchen to make supper for the family. She had bought three pounds of spareribs. Now she opened a package of baked beans and seasoning mix. She coated the ribs with the contents of one of the little bags inside. Then she put the uncooked beans in another bag, added water, added the seasoning from another little bag, and put the ribs on top of the floating beans. Then she twisted the large bag closed, put it in a baking dish, and slid the whole thing into a preheated oven. It would sit there for an hour and a half, and then the Schumacher family would eat it. Between now and then, though, Cathy had to shuck and boil the corn.

At suppertime, just as the timer was going off on the oven, Victor came home. "I'm late, Cathy," he called from the living room.

"I know," she said.

"What's for supper?"

"Ribs and beans."

"Terrific. Got my drink?"

"Sure," said Cathy, wiping her hands on the dish towel that hung on the refrigerator door handle. "Here." She poured him an apéritif, a small glass of Amaretto, an Italian liqueur. She thought it was funny, Victor drinking—sipping—at Amaretto and sitting down to eat ribs and baked beans from a packaged mix. With the meal they all drank Coke.

After dinner, Cathy told Leslie to clear off the table. Victor explained that he had quite a bit of work to do before morning; Cathy just nodded and said nothing. There was no hint of the objectless fears that had bothered her all day. She washed the dishes and put them away. Then she tied up all the garbage in a plastic bag and told Leslie to take it downstairs. After that, there was nothing else to do. Cathy put some piano sonatas

131

on the stereo and sat by herself in the living room. There were things she could have done, of course; she could have looked through her professional journals, she could have prepared her lecture for the next class, she could have written letters. But she had no energy for that kind of thing. She felt anxious, even expectant of some strange event. She didn't know yet what she was waiting for, but she felt certain that whatever it might be, it would happen soon.

When it came time for the evening news, Cathy called Victor, but he said that he hadn't finished his work. Leslie was already in bed. Cathy watched the news alone.

"Good evening," said the newscaster, "my name is Gil Monahan, and it's time for the 'Ten O'Clock News Wrapup.' Before the headlines, I'd like to tell Mrs. Cathy Schumacher that she ought to be careful. You're liable to cause yourself more trouble in the future if you try to avoid it now. And here's the news. In Harrisburg this evening—"

Cathy gave a little, stifled shriek. She went to the television and turned it off. "I ought to call the station," she thought. "I ought to find out what that was all about." She stood in the middle of the living-room floor, indecisive. At last she decided against calling the station. That might be just the kind of thing she was being warned against. "Oh, God," she thought, "now I'm really taking it all seriously." That night, in bed, she had an impossible time trying to fall asleep. Victor, asleep beside her, looked so peaceful. Cathy recalled that even up to the night before, she herself had been so undisturbed. Now it seemed unlikely to her that she would be allowed to regain her self-control.

She stared at the shadows on the ceiling, feeling the tension in her grow, worse than that morning in her office, worse than in the supermarket, much worse than even while she watched the newscaster. She thought of taking a pill to make her sleep, but by then it was already three o'clock and she'd stay asleep until almost noon. She had responsibilities.

She was in her office the next morning at ten o'clock. She told herself a number of trite things, all supposed to make her feel better and to minimize her remembrance of the things that had happened the day before. Time goes on, she told herself, and the memory of those odd things will fade. Work hard, she told herself, and you won't have time to think. She picked up one of her pupils' compositions, which she had been unable to read the previous day. She got through the same three pages she had read before, then continued. The poem on which the paper was based was only a few hundred lines long; the paper seemed to go on for volumes. It had gotten to the point in her teaching career where she had given up looking for originality, for insight, even for logical coherence. She knew these were impossible things to expect. She found herself giving higher grades to papers that were typed neatly and written with a certain familiarity with the English language. She didn't ask a lot. She had learned that it was pointless to try.

On page eight of the manuscript, Cathy read this line:

This area is completely under water today.[9]

Without thinking about what had happened in a similar circumstance the day before, Cathy looked at the bottom of the page to check the pupil's source. She read:

[9]*Mrs. Schumacher, if you went home right now, you'd find your husband in bed with the woman from apartment 2F.*

"Well," thought Cathy, "at least they're not being cryptic any more." She stared at the page for a moment, then put the paper on her desk. She looked out of her window, across the common. The trees which in spring were so lovely now looked dead forever; among them on the common were three spired churches. To Cathy they looked empty and cold. The sky was cloudy, and the lonely, slow-moving figures across College Street added to a picture of desolation she had never seen before through that window. With a start she returned her attention to her office, to her work, to the paper she was supposed to be reading. She picked it up again. The footnote was still there, still warning her, still rather embarrassedly calling her attention to a situation she should know about. Who wrote this paper anyway? She turned back to the first page; it was done by Randy Irons, the blond, tall young man who sat far in the back. How could he know such an intimate thing about Victor? Well, it was possible, Cathy supposed, but then, how could Mr. Irons *and* Gil Monahan on the news know? And the authors of the movie-magazine article and the article in the Journal?

Did everybody in the world know, except her? Isn't that what they always said, that the spouse was the last to find out?

Maybe so, Cathy thought, but surely they didn't make public announcements for the benefit of everyone else in the same position. Not on the nighttime news. Not in pupils' homework papers or magazines that the oblivious subject generally never read. Cathy stood up and went to Wally's office, carrying the paper Randy Irons had so thoughtfully written.

"Wally?" she called, outside his office.

"Cathy?"

"Yeah. Are you busy?"

Wally came to the door and gestured that she should come in. "In the last two years, have you ever known me to be busy?" he asked.

"No," she said.

"There. What's the matter?"

"Do you remember yesterday?" asked Cathy. She took a deep breath; she felt like crying, and she felt foolish.

"Barely," said Wally. "It's already beginning to fade into last week."

"I had something I wanted to talk to you about, and then I didn't."

"Right," said Wally, suddenly serious, "I remember."

"Well, it keeps happening. Yesterday I thought, well, maybe it was a joke or something, but now I think I'm going crazy or I already am crazy or something."

"You haven't done a very good job of explaining."

"I'm sorry, Wally. Did you see the Channel Five news last night?"

"I watch Channel Two."

"Oh. Gil Monahan started off the newscast by telling me—me, personally, Mrs. Cathy Schumacher—to be careful. That's not very professional, is it?"

"No," said Wally thoughtfully.

"Yesterday, while I was waiting in line at the supermarket, I picked up one of those teen movie magazines. The first article I saw had an opening sentence that said something like, 'Cathy Schumacher, you have to listen!' That must have been set in type months ago, just so I could see it yesterday in Egerton's. And the thing I mentioned before lunch was the same kind of thing, in my *Journal of the Institute for Early English Studies*. Last night I was really scared. And today it's even worse."

"Did you try verifying any of these things?"

"No."

"Of course not. You're too afraid to find out that they're real, and you're even more afraid to find out they're delusions. You only have two choices. You could ask the people whom you think are communicating with you, and find out why they're doing it the way they are, or you could go tell the whole thing to a doctor. I'll bet it's a pretty common clinical syndrome. You probably know exactly what it all means. You're just masking the knowledge from your conscious thoughts, and your subconscious is intruding. These, uh, manifestations are just a way of you having to make some discovery yourself on a conscious level. You can put the responsibility onto these other people."

Cathy slid Irons' theme across the desk. "Look at the footnote on the bottom of the page," she said. Wally read it, turned to the first page of the paper, glanced through the rest of it, and said nothing. He handed the paper back to Cathy.

"Well," he said after an uncomfortable moment of silence, "have you tried calling home?"

"No," said Cathy.

"I can understand that. Do you want me to?"

"No," said Cathy, "I'll do it. I'll go back to my office now."

"Is there something I can do? I don't know what to say."

"Don't worry about it," said Cathy. "I can handle it now, I think. I just wanted to make sure that I wasn't completely nuts."

"You're not nuts. Of course, you could be editing this whole conversation. You could be so crazy that I might be talking about fly fishing, and you'd be hearing what you want. But then we get into the arguments about perceiving reality, and it's not even lunchtime yet."

"Thanks," said Cathy.

In her own office again, Cathy sat down and stared

at the telephone. Wally had made a good point, even though he was probably joking. She would never really be able to know how much of what she saw and heard was true; she might not in fact even have gone to his office. She couldn't accept his verification. If she disallowed the premise that her mind might be altering what her senses were telling her, then no one else's words had any validity. Including a psychiatrist's. How could Cathy know when it was her own mind deceiving her? Could she actually *prove* that Wally had seen the footnote in Randy Irons' paper, and that it said to him what it said to her? From now on, Cathy knew that she could only trust what her own mind told her that her own senses were perceiving. And she'd have to go on on that basis. There wasn't anything else.

But maybe she ought to see a doctor, anyway.

She picked up the telephone, dialed nine, got an outside line, and called her home number. She listened to the phone ring, over and over, six times, seven times, eight. Then Victor answered. Cathy felt cold suddenly. "Hello, Victor?" she said.

"Yes, Cathy. Anything wrong?"

"No, no. Of course not. Why are you home?"

Victor paused for a moment. "I got sick at work today. Maybe I worked too hard last night. I came home and went to bed. Why did you call? Who did you think would be here?"

Cathy realized that she had made a mistake. "Oh, I called your office and Miss Brant said that you'd gone home. I was worried, so I called to see if you want me to come take care of you."

"No," said Victor, "that's all right. I don't feel that bad. There isn't anything you could do, anyway. I think I'll just take a nap."

"All right, honey," said Cathy. "Feel better. Remember that I love you."

137

There was another silence. "Me too," said Victor after a while. Cathy held the receiver, shook her head, and hung up. She walked around her little office, nervously doing meaningless tidying things. She felt helpless. That was what helped save her. She didn't like feeling helpless.

"An effort of will," she thought. "That's all it takes. All right, subconscious, you win. I'm aware. So what?" She sat down again and picked up the other student paper. She read a couple of pages, until she found the first footnote. Almost eagerly, she looked at the bottom of the page. The footnote said:

¹*These things happen, Mrs. Schumacher.*

These things happen, indeed, she thought. Somehow, she felt relieved. She took the page to the English Department Xerox machine, made a copy of it, and cut the bottom of the page into a neat rectangle. Then she put on her coat and went to the drugstore across the city common. She bought a cheap black wood frame and returned to her office. She framed the piece of the Xerox copy and hung the frame on the wall. So many things would have to be done, have to be thought, have to be said in the next few days. The sentiment in the frame made her feel better. It returned to her a sense of security in the continuity of reality. She called Wally on the phone. "Hello," she said.

"Hello," he said, his voice sounding worried. "How are you?"

"Better and better," said Cathy. "I want to ask you a favor. I want to go out now and get really drunk."

"You don't do that."

"I need the practice."

"Your problem?"

"Sure," she said.

"Do you want to talk about it?" asked Wally quietly.

"Oh, no," said Cathy. "Not at all."

"Well, look," said Wally, "getting drunk certainly isn't the most constructive way of tackling a problem."

Cathy looked at the frame on the wall. From that distance, the footnote inside was unreadable. She laughed. "Who gives a good goddamn?" she said. After a moment, Wally laughed too.

Ambrose Bierce defined history as "An account mostly false, of events mostly unimportant, which are brought about by rulers mostly knaves, and soldiers mostly fools." Unfortunately, this has frequently been true also of sf writers' tales of "future history": planet-shaking battles fought by jut-jawed heroes while the vast majority of humans live their lives as best they can somewhere in the unrecorded background.

Here Gene Wolfe, who won a Nebula Award for "The Death of Dr. Island" in **Universe 3**, tells of a future when endless wars are steadily destroying civilization . . . but the battle is only thunder in the distance; his story is about the non-combatants who try to preserve what they can of past technology. (Nor does Wolfe forget that there are knaves and fools among the nonheroes too.)

THE MARVELOUS BRASS CHESSPLAYING AUTOMATON

Gene Wolfe

Each day Lame Hans sits with his knees against the bars, playing chess with the machine. Though I have seen the game often, I have never learned to play, but I watch them as I sweep. It is a beautiful game, and Lame Hans has told me of its beginnings in the great ages now past; for that reason I always feel a sympathy toward the little pawns with their pencils and wrenches and plain clothing, each figure representing many generations of those whose labor built the great bishops that split the skies in the days of the old wars.

I feel pity for Lame Hans also. He talks to me when I bring his food, and sometimes when I am cleaning the jail. Let me tell you his story, as I have learned it in the many days since the police drew poor Gretchen out and laid her in the dust of the street. Lame Hans would never tell you himself—for all that big, bulging head, his tongue is slow and halting when he speaks of his own affairs.

It was last summer during the truce that the showman's cart was driven into our village. For a month not a drop of rain had fallen; each day at noon Father Karl rang the church bells, and women went in to pray for rain for their husbands' crops. After dark, many of these same women met to form lines and circles on the slopes of the Schlossberg, the mountain that was once a great building. The lines and circles are supposed to influence the Weatherwatchers, whose winking lights pass so swiftly through the starry sky. For myself, I do not believe it. What men ever made a machine that could see a few old women on the mountainside at night?

So it was when the cart of Herr Heitzmann the mountebank came. The sun was down, but the street still so hot that the dogs would not bark for fear of fainting, and the dust rolled away from the wheels in waves, like grain when foxes run through the fields.

This cart was shorter than a farm wagon, but very high, with such a roof as a house has. The sides had been painted, and even I, who do not play, but have so often watched Albricht the moneylender play Father Karl, or Doctor Eckardt play Burgermeister Landsteiner, recognized the mighty figures of the Queen-Computers who lead the armies of the field of squares into battle; and the haughty King-Generals who command, and if they fall, bring down all.

A small, bent man drove. He had a head large enough for a giant—that was Lame Hans, but I paid little attention to him, not knowing that he and I would be companions here in the jail where I work. Beside him sat Heitzmann the mountebank, and it was he who took one's eyes, which was as he intended. He was tall and thin, with a sharp chin and a large nose and snapping black eyes. He had velvet trousers and a fine hat which sweat had stained around the band, and long locks of dark hair that hung from under it at odd angles so that one knew he used the finger-comb when he woke, as drunkards do who find themselves beneath a bench. When the small man brought the cart through the innyard gate, I rose from my seat on the jail steps and went across to the inn parlor. And it was a fortunate thing I did so, because it was in this way that I chanced to see the famous game between the brass machine and Professor Baumeister.

Haven't I mentioned Professor Baumeister before? Have you not noticed that in a village such as ours there are always a dozen celebrities? Always a man who is strong (with us that is Willi Schacht, the smith's apprentice), one who eats a great deal, a learned man like Doctor Eckardt, a ladies' man, and so on. But for all these people to be properly admired, there must also be a distinguished visitor to whom to point them out, and here in Oder Spree that is Professor Baumeister, because our village lies midway between the University and Furstenwald, and it is here that he spends the night whenever he journeys from one to the other, much to the enrichment of Scheer the innkeeper. The fact of the matter is that Professor Baumeister has become one of our celebrities himself, only by spending the night here so often. With his broad brown beard and fine coat and tall hat and leather riding breeches, he gives the parlor of our inn the air of a gentlemen's club.

I have heard that it is often the case that the beginning of the greatest drama is as casual as any commonplace event. So it was that night. The inn was full of off-duty soldiers drinking beer, and because of the heat all the windows were thrown open, though a dozen candles were burning. Professor Baumeister was deep in conversation with Doctor Eckardt: something about the war. Herr Heitzmann the mountebank—though I did not know what to call him then—had already gotten his half liter when I came in, and was standing at the bar.

At last, when Professor Baumeister paused to emphasize some point, Herr Heitzmann leaned over to them, and in the most offhand way asked a question. It was peculiar, but the whole room seemed to grow silent as he spoke, so that he could be heard everywhere, though it was no more than a whisper. He said: "I wonder if I might venture to ask you gentlemen— you both appear to be learned men—if, to the best of your knowledge, there still exists even one of those great computational machines which were perhaps the most extraordinary—I trust you will agree with me?—creations of the age now past."

Professor Baumeister said at once: "No sir. Not one remains."

"You feel certain of this?"

"My dear sir," said Professor Baumeister, "you must understand that those devices were dependent upon a supply of replacement parts consisting of the most delicate subminiature electronic components. These have not been produced now for over a hundred years— indeed, some of them have been unavailable longer."

"Ah," Herr Heitzmann said (mostly to himself, it

143

seemed, but you could hear him in the kitchen). "Then I have the only one."

Professor Baumeister attempted to ignore this amazing remark, as not having been addressed to himself; but Doctor Eckardt, who is of an inquisitive disposition, said boldly: "You have such a machine, Herr . . . ?"

"Heitzmann. Originally of Berlin, now come from Zurich. And you, my good sir?"

Doctor Eckardt introduced himself, and Professor Baumeister too, and Herr Heitzmann clasped them by the hand. Then the doctor said to Professor Baumeister: "You are certain that no computers remain in existence, my friend?"

The professor said: "I am referring to working computers—machines in operating condition. There are plenty of old hulks in museums, of course."

Herr Heitzmann sighed, and pulled out a chair and sat down at the table with them, bringing his beer. "Would it not be sad," he said, "if those world-ruling machines were lost to mankind forever?"

Professor Baumeister said dryly: "They based their extrapolations on numbers. That worked well enough as long as money, which is easily measured numerically, was the principal motivating force in human affairs. But as time progressed, human actions became responsive instead to a multitude of incommensurable vectors; the computers' predictions failed, the civilization they had shaped collapsed, and parts for the machines were no longer obtainable or desired."

"How fascinating!" Herr Heitzmann exclaimed. "Do you know, I have never heard it explained in quite that way. You have provided me, for the first time, with an explanation for the survival of my own machine."

Doctor Eckardt said, "You have a working computer, then?"

"I do. You see, mine is a specialized device. It was not designed, like the computers the learned professor spoke of just now, to predict human actions. It plays chess."

"And where do you keep this wonderful machine?" By this time everyone else in the room had fallen silent. Even Scheer took care not to allow the glasses he was drying to clink; and Gretchen, the fat blond serving girl who usually cracked jokes with the soldiers and banged down their plates, moved through the pipe smoke among the tables as quietly as the moon moves in a cloudy sky.

"Outside," Herr Heitzmann replied. "In my conveyance. I am taking it to Dresden."

"And it plays chess."

"It has never been defeated."

"Are you aware," Professor Baumeister inquired sardonically, "that to program a computer to play chess—to play well—was considered one of the most difficult problems? That many judged that it was never actually solved, and that those machines which most closely approached acceptable solutions were never so small as to be portable?"

"Nevertheless," Herr Heitzmann declared, "I have such a machine."

"My friend, I do not believe you."

"I take it you are a player yourself," Herr Heitzmann said. "Such a learned man could hardly be otherwise. Very well. As I said a moment ago, my machine is outside." His hand touched the table between Professor Baumeister's glass and his own, and when it came away five gold kilomarks stood there in a neat stack. "I will lay these on the outcome of the game, if you will play my machine tonight."

"Done," said Professor Baumeister.

"I must see your money."

"You will accept a draft on Streicher's, in Fursten-wald?"

And so it was settled. Doctor Eckardt held the stakes, and six men volunteered to carry the machine into the inn parlor under Herr Heitzmann's direction.

Six were not too many, though the machine was not as large as might have been expected—not more than a hundred and twenty centimeters high, with a base, as it might be, a meter on a side. The sides and top were all of brass, set with many dials and other devices no one understood.

When it was at last in place, Professor Baumeister viewed it from all sides and smiled. "This is not a computer," he said.

"My dear friend," said Herr Heitzmann, "you are mistaken."

"It is several computers. There are two keyboards and a portion of a third. There are even two nameplates, and one of these dials once belonged to a radio."

Herr Heitzmann nodded. "It was assembled at the very close of the period, for one purpose only—to play chess."

"You still contend that this machine can play?"

"I contend more. That it will win."

"Very well. Bring a board."

"That is not necessary," Herr Heitzmann said. He pulled a knob at the front of the machine, and a whole section swung forward, as the door of a vegetable bin does in a scullery. But the top of this bin was not open as though to receive the vegetables: it was instead a chessboard, with the white squares of brass, and the black of smoky glass, and on the board, standing in formation and ready to play, were two armies of chess-men such as no one in our village had ever seen, tall

146

metal figures so stately they might have been sculptured apostles in a church, one army of brass and the other of some dark metal. "You may play white," Herr Heitzmann said. "That is generally considered an advantage."

Professor Baumeister nodded, advanced the white king's pawn two squares, and drew a chair up to the board. By the time he had seated himself the machine had replied, moving so swiftly that no one saw by what mechanism the piece had been shifted.

The next time Professor Baumeister acted more slowly, and everyone watched, eager to see the machine's countermove. It came the moment the professor had set his piece in its new position—the black queen slid forward silently, with nothing to propel it.

After ten moves Professor Baumeister said, "There is a man inside."

Herr Heitzmann smiled. "I see why you say that, my friend. Your position on the board is precarious."

"I insist that the machine be opened for my examination."

"I suppose you would say that if a man were concealed inside, the bet would be canceled." Herr Heitzmann had ordered a second glass of beer, and was leaning against the bar watching the game.

"Of course. My bet was that a machine could not defeat me. I am well aware that certain human players can."

"But conversely, if there is no man in the machine, the bet stands?"

"Certainly."

"Very well." Herr Heitzmann walked to the machine, twisted four catches on one side, and with the help of some onlookers removed the entire panel. It was of brass, like the rest of the machine but, because the metal was thin, not so heavy as it appeared.

There was more room inside than might have been thought, yet withal a considerable amount of mechanism: things like shingles the size of little tabletops, all covered with patterns like writing (Lame Hans has told me since that these are called circuit cards). And gears and motors and the like.

When Professor Baumeister had poked among all these mechanical parts for half a minute, Herr Heitzmann asked: "Are you satisfied?"

"Yes," answered Professor Baumeister, straightening up. "There is no one in there."

"But *I* am not," said Herr Heitzmann, and he walked with long strides to the other side of the machine. Everyone crowded around him as he released the catches on that side, lifted away the panel, and stood it against the wall. "Now," he said, "you can see completely through my machine—isn't that right? Look, do you see Doctor Eckardt? Do you see me? Wave to us."

"I am satisfied," Professor Baumeister said. "Let us go on with the game."

"The machine has already taken its move. You may think about your next one while these gentlemen help me replace the panels."

Professor Baumeister was beaten in twenty-two moves. Albricht the moneylender then asked if he could play without betting, and when this was refused by Herr Heitzmann, bet a kilomark and was beaten in fourteen moves. Herr Heitzmann asked then if anyone else would play, and when no one replied, requested that the same men who had carried the machine into the inn assist him in putting it away again.

"Wait," said Professor Baumeister.

Herr Heitzmann smiled. "You mean to play again?"

"No. I want to buy your machine. On behalf of the University."

Herr Heitzmann sat down and looked serious. "I doubt that I could sell it to you. I had hoped to make a good sum in Dresden before selling it there."

"Five hundred kilomarks."

Herr Heitzmann shook his head. "That is a fair proposition," he said, "and I thank you for making it. But I cannot accept."

"Seven hundred and fifty," Professor Baumeister said. "That is my final offer."

"In gold?"

"In a draft on an account the University maintains in Furstenwald—you can present it there for gold the first thing in the morning."

"You must understand," said Herr Heitzmann, "that the machine requires a certain amount of care, or it will not perform properly."

"I am buying it as is," said Professor Baumeister. "As it stands here before us."

"Done, then," said Herr Heitzmann, and he put out his hand.

The board was folded away, and six stout fellows carried the machine into the professor's room for safekeeping, where he remained with it for an hour or more. When he returned to the inn parlor at last, Doctor Eckardt asked if he had been playing chess again.

Professor Baumeister nodded. "Three games."

"Did you win?"

"No, I lost them all. Where is the showman?"

"Gone," said Father Karl, who was sitting near them. "He left as soon as you took the machine to your room."

Doctor Eckardt said, "I thought he planned to stay the night here."

"So did I," said Father Karl. "And I confess I believed the machine would not function without him. I was surprised to hear that our friend the professor had been playing in private."

Just then a small, twisted man, with a large head crowned with wild black hair, limped into the inn parlor. It was Lame Hans, but no one knew that then. He asked Scheer the innkeeper for a room.

Scheer smiled. "Sitting rooms on the first floor are a hundred marks," he said. He could see by Lame Hans's worn clothes that he could not afford a sitting room.

"Something cheaper."

"My regular rooms are thirty marks. Or I can let you have a garret for ten."

Hans rented a garret room, and ordered a meal of beer, tripe, and kraut. That was the last time anyone except Gretchen noticed Lame Hans that night.

And now I must leave off recounting what I myself saw, and tell many things that rest solely on the testimony of Lame Hans, given to me while he ate his potato soup in his cell. But I believe Lame Hans to be an honest fellow; and as he no longer, as he says, cares much to live, he has no reason to lie.

One thing is certain. Lame Hans and Gretchen the serving girl fell in love that night. Just how it happened I cannot say—I doubt that Lame Hans himself knows. She was sent to prepare the cot in his garret. Doubtless she was tired after drawing beer in the parlor all day, and was happy to sit for a few moments and talk with him. Perhaps she smiled—she was always a girl who smiled a great deal—and laughed at some bitter joke he made. And as for Lame Hans, how many blue-eyed girls could ever have smiled at him, with his big head and twisted leg?

In the morning the machine would not play chess.

Professor Baumeister sat before it for a long time,

arranging the pieces and making first one opening and then another, and tinkering with the mechanism; but nothing happened.

And then, when the morning was half gone, Lame Hans came into his room. "You paid a great deal of money for this machine," he said, and sat down in the best chair.

"Were you in the inn parlor last night?" asked Professor Baumeister. "Yes, I paid a great deal: seven hundred and fifty kilomarks."

"I was there," said Lame Hans. "You must be a very rich man to be able to afford such a sum."

"It was the University's money," explained Professor Baumeister.

"Ah," said Lame Hans. "Then it will be embarrassing for you if the machine does not play."

"It does play," said the professor. "I played three games with it last night after it was brought here."

"You must learn to make better use of your knights," Lame Hans told him, "and to attack on both sides of the board at once. In the second game you played well until you lost the queen's rook; then you went to pieces."

The professor sat down, and for a moment said nothing. And then: "You are the operator of the machine. I was correct in the beginning; I should have known."

Lame Hans looked out the window.

"How did you move the pieces—by radio? I suppose there must still be radio-control equipment in existence somewhere."

"I was inside," Lame Hans said. "I'll show you sometime; it's not important. What will you tell the University?"

"That I was swindled, I suppose. I have some money of my own, and I will try to pay back as much as I can out of that—and I own two houses in Fursten-wald that can be sold."

"Do you smoke?" asked Lame Hans, and he took out his short pipe, and a bag of tobacco.

"Only after dinner," said the professor, "and not often then."

"I find it calms my nerves," said Lame Hans. "That is why I suggested it to you. I do not have a second pipe, but I can offer you some of my tobacco, which is very good. You might buy a clay from the innkeeper here."

"No, thank you. I fear I must abandon such little pleasures for a long time to come."

"Not necessarily," said Lame Hans. "Go ahead, buy that pipe. This is good Turkish tobacco—would you believe, to look at me, that I know a great deal about tobacco? It has been my only luxury."

"If you are the one who played chess with me last night," Professor Baumeister said, "I would be willing to believe that you know a great deal about anything. You play like the devil himself."

"I know a great deal about more than tobacco. Would you like to get your money back?"

And so it was that that very afternoon (if it can be credited), the mail coach carried away bills printed in large black letters. These said:

IN THE VILLAGE OF ODER SPREE

BEFORE THE INN OF THE GOLDEN APPLES

ON SATURDAY

AT 9:00 O'CLOCK

THE MARVELOUS BRASS CHESSPLAYING AUTOMATON

WILL

BE ON DISPLAY

FREE TO EVERYONE

Now, you will think from what I have told you that
Lame Hans was a cocky fellow, but that is not the
case, though like many of us who are small of stature
he pretended to be self-reliant when he was among
men taller than he. The truth is that though he did not
show it he was very frightened when he met Herr Heitzmann (as the two of them had arranged earlier that he
should) in a certain malodorous tavern near the
Schwarzthor in Furstenwald.

"So there you are, my friend," said Herr Heitzmann.
"How did it go?"

"Terribly," Lame Hans replied as though he felt
nothing. "I was locked up in that brass snuffbox for
half the night, and had to play twenty games with that
fool of a scholar. And when at last I got out, I couldn't
get a ride here and had to walk most of the way on this
bad leg of mine. I trust it was comfortable on the cart
seat? The horse didn't give you too much trouble?"

"I'm sorry you've had a poor time of it, but now you
can relax. There's nothing more to do until he's convinced the machine is broken and irreparable."

Lame Hans looked at him as though in some surprise. "You didn't see the signs? They are posted everywhere."

"What signs?"

"He's offering to bet two thousand kilomarks that no
one can beat the machine."

Herr Heitzmann shrugged. "He will discover that it
is inoperative before the contest, and cancel it."

"He could not cancel after the bet was made," said
Lame Hans. "Particularly if there were a proviso that

153

if either were unable to play, the bet was forfeited. Some upright citizen would be selected to hold the stakes, naturally."

"I don't suppose he could at that," said Herr Heitzmann, taking a swallow of schnapps from the glass before him. "However, he wouldn't bet *me*—he'd think I knew some way to influence the machine. Still, he's never seen *you*."

"Just what I've been thinking myself," said Lame Hans, "on my hike."

"It's a little out of your line."

"If you'll put up the cash, I'd be willing to go a little out of my line for my tenth of that kind of money. But what is there to do? I make the bet, find someone to hold the stakes, and stand ready to play on Saturday morning. I could even offer to play him—for a smaller bet—to give him a chance to get some of his own back. That is, if he has anything left after paying off. It would make it seem more sporting."

"You're certain you could beat him?"

"I can beat anybody—you know that. Besides, I beat him a score of times yesterday; the game you saw was just the first."

Herr Heitzmann ducked under the threatening edge of a tray carried by an overenthusiastic waiter. "All the same," he said, "when he discovers it won't work . . ."

"I could even spend a bit of time in the machine. That's no problem. It's in a first-floor room, with a window that won't lock."

And so Lame Hans left for our village again, this time considerably better dressed and with two thousand kilomarks in his pocket. Herr Heitzmann, with his appearance considerably altered by a plastiskin mask, left also, an hour later, to keep an eye on the two thousand.

154

"But," the professor said when Lame Hans and he were comfortably ensconced in his sitting room again, with pipes in their mouths and glasses in their hands and a plate of sausage on the table, "but who is going to operate the machine for us? Wouldn't it be easier if you simply didn't appear? Then you would forfeit."

"And Heitzmann would kill me," said Lame Hans.

"He didn't strike me as the type."

"He would hire it done," Hans said positively. "Whenever he got the cash. There are deserters about who are happy enough to do that kind of work for drinking money. For that matter, there are soldiers who aren't deserters who'll do it—men on detached duty of one kind and another. When you've spent all winter slaughtering Russians, one more body doesn't make much difference." He blew a smoke ring, then ran the long stem of his clay pipe through it as though he were driving home a bayonet. "But if I play the machine and lose, he'll only think you figured things out and got somebody to work it, and that I'm not as good as he supposed. Then he won't want anything more to do with me."

"All right, then."

"A tobacconist should do well in this village, don't you think? I had in mind that little shop two doors down from here. When the coaches stop, the passengers will see my sign; there should be many who'll want to fill their pouches."

"Gretchen prefers to stay here, I suppose."

Lame Hans nodded. "It doesn't matter to me. I've been all over, and when you've been all over, it's all the same."

Like everyone else in the village, and for fifty kilometers around, I had seen the professor's posters, and I went to bed Friday night full of pleasant anticipation.

Lame Hans has told me that he retired in the same frame of mind, after a couple of glasses of good plum brandy in the inn parlor with the professor. He and the professor had to appear strangers and antagonists in public, as will be readily seen; but this did not prevent them from eating and drinking together while they discussed arrangements for the match, which was to be held—with the permission of Burgermeister Landsteiner—in the village street, where an area for the players had been cordoned off and high benches erected for the spectators.

Hans woke (so he has told me) when it was still dark, thinking that he had heard thunder. Then the noise came again, and he knew it must be the artillery, the big siege guns, firing at the Russians trapped in Kostrzyn. The army had built wood-fired steam tractors to pull those guns—he had seen them in Wriezen—and now the soldiers were talking about putting armor on the tractors and mounting cannon, so the knights of the chessboard would exist in reality once more.

The firing continued, booming across the dry plain, and he went to the window to see if he could make out the flashes, but could not. He put on a thin shirt and a pair of cotton trousers (for though the sun was not yet up, it was as hot as if the whole of Brandenburg had been thrust into a furnace) and went into the street to look at the empty shop in which he planned to set up his tobacco business. A squadron of *Ritters* galloped through the village, doubtless on their way to the siege. Lame Hans shouted, "What do you mean to do? Ride your horses against the walls?" but they ignored him. Now that the truce was broken, Von Koblenz's army would soon be advancing up the Oder Valley, Lame Hans thought. The Russians were said to have been preparing powered balloons to assist in the defense,

156

and this hot summer weather, when the air seemed never to stir, would favor their use. He decided that if he were the Commissar, he would allow Von Koblenz to reach Glogow, and then ...

But he was not the Commissar. He went back into the inn and smoked his pipe until Frau Scheer came down to prepare his breakfast. Then he went to the professor's room where the machine was kept. Gretchen was already waiting there.

"Now then," Professor Baumeister said, "I understand that the two of you have it all worked out between you." And Gretchen nodded solemnly, so that her plump chin looked like a soft little pillow pressed against her throat.

"It is quite simple," said Lame Hans. "Gretchen does not know how to play, but I have worked out the moves for her and drawn them on a sheet of paper, and we have practiced in my room with a board. We will run through it once here when she is in the machine, then there will be nothing more to do."

"Is it a short game? It won't do for her to become confused."

"She will win in fourteen moves," Lame Hans promised. "But still it is unusual. I don't think anyone has done it before. You will see in a moment."

To Gretchen, Professor Baumeister said: "You're sure you won't be mixed up? Everything depends on you."

The girl shook her head, making her blond braids dance. "No, Herr Professor." She drew a folded piece of paper from her bosom. "I have it all here, and as my Hans told you, we have practiced in his room, where no one could see us."

"You aren't afraid?"

"When I am going to marry Hans, and be mistress of a fine shop? Oh, no, Herr Professor—for that I would do much worse things than to hide in this thing that looks like a stove, and play a game."

"We are ready, then," the professor said. "Hans, you still have not explained how it is that a person can hide in there, when the sides can be removed allowing people to look through the machinery. And I confess I still don't understand how it can be done, or how the pieces are moved."

"Here," said Lame Hans, and he pulled out the board as Herr Heitzmann had done in the inn parlor. "Now will you assist me in removing the left side? You should learn the way it comes loose, Professor—someday you may have to do it yourself." (The truth was that he was not strong enough to handle the big brass sheet by himself, and did not wish to be humiliated before Gretchen.)

"I had forgotten how much empty space there is inside," Professor Baumeister said when they had it off. "It looks more impossible than ever."

"It is simple, like all good tricks," Lame Hans told him. "And it is the sign of a good trick that it is the thing that makes it appear difficult that makes it easy. Here is where the chessboard is, you see, when it is folded up. But when it is unfolded, the panel under it swings out on a hinge to support it, and there are sides, so that a triangular space is formed."

The professor nodded and said, "I remember thinking when I played you that it looked like a potato bin, with the chessboard laid over the top."

"Exactly," Lame Hans continued. "The space is not noticeable when the machine is open, because this circuit card is just in front of it. But see here." And he released a little catch at the top of the circuit card, and pivoted it up to show the empty space behind it. "I am in the machine when it is carried in, but when Heitzmann pulls out the board, I lift this and fit myself

158

under it; then, when the machine is opened for inspection, I am out of view. I can look up through the dark glass of the black squares, and because the pieces are so tall, I can make out their positions. But because it is bright outside, but dim where I am, I cannot be seen."

"I understand," said the professor. "But will Gretchen have enough light in there to read her piece of paper?"

"That was why I wanted to hold the match in the street. With the board in sunshine, she will be able to see her paper clearly."

Gretchen was on her knees, looking at the space behind the circuit card. "It is very small in there," she said.

"It is big enough," said Lame Hans. "Do you have the magnet?" And then to the professor: "The pieces are moved by moving a magnet under them. The white pieces are brass, but the black ones are of iron, and the magnet gives them a sliding motion that is very impressive."

"I know," said the professor, remembering that he had felt a twinge of uneasiness whenever the machine had shifted a piece. "Gretchen, see if you can get inside."

The poor girl did the best she could, but encountered the greatest difficulty in wedging herself into the small space under the board. Work in the kitchen of the inn had provided her with many opportunities to snatch a mouthful of pastry or a choice potato dumpling or a half stein of dark beer, and she had availed herself of most of them—with the result that she possessed a lush and blooming figure of the sort that appeals to men like Lame Hans, who, having been withered before birth by the isotopes of the old wars, are themselves thin and small by nature. But though full breasts like ripe melons, and a rounded, comfortable stomach and generous hips, may be pleasant things to look at when the moonlight comes in the bedroom window, they are not really well-suited to folding up in a little three-cornered space under a chessboard; and in the end, poor Gretchen was forced to remove her gown, and her shift as well, before she could cram herself, with much gasping and grunting, into it.

An hour later, Willi Schacht the smith's apprentice and five other men carried the machine out into the street and set it in the space that had been cordoned off for the players, and if they noticed the extra weight, they did not complain of it. And there the good people who had come to see the match looked at the machine, and fanned themselves, and said that they were glad they weren't in the army on a day like this—because what must it be to serve one of those big guns, which get hot enough to poach an egg after half a dozen shots, even in ordinary weather? And between moppings and fannings they talked about the machine, and the mysterious Herr Zimmer (that was the name Lame Hans had given) who was going to play it for two hundred gold kilomarks.

Nine chimes sounded from the old clock in the steeple of Father Karl's church, and Herr Zimmer did not appear.

Doctor Eckardt, who had been chosen again to hold the stakes, came forward and whispered for some time with Professor Baumeister. The professor (if the truth were known) was beginning to believe that perhaps Lame Hans had decided it was best to forfeit after all—though in fact, if anyone had looked, he would have seen Lame Hans sitting at the bar of the inn at that very moment, having a pleasant nip of plum

160

brandy and then another, while he allowed the suspense to build up as a good showman should.

At last Doctor Eckardt climbed upon a chair and announced: "It is now nearly ten. When the bet was made, it was agreed by both parties that if either failed to appear—or appearing, failed to play—the other should be declared the winner. If the worthy stranger, Herr Zimmer, does not make an appearance before ten minutes past ten, I intend to award the money entrusted to me to our respected acquaintance Professor Baumeister."

There was a murmur of excitement at this, but just when the clock began to strike, Lame Hans called from the door of the inn: "WAIT!" Then hats were thrown into the air, and women stood on toetips to see; and fathers lifted their children up as the lame Herr Zimmer made his way down the steps of the inn and took his place in the chair that had been arranged in front of the board.

"Are you ready to begin?" said Doctor Eckardt.

"I am," said Lame Hans, and opened.

The first five moves were made just as they had been rehearsed. But in the sixth, in which Gretchen was to have slid her queen half across the board, the piece stopped a square short.

Any ordinary player would have been dismayed, but Lame Hans was not. He only put his chin on his hand, and contrived (though wishing he had not drunk the brandy) a series of moves within the frame of the fourteen-move game, by which he should lose despite the queen's being out of position. He made the first of these moves; and black moved the queen again, this time in a way that was completely different from anything on the paper Hans had given Gretchen. *She was deceiving me when she said she did not know how to play*, he thought to himself. *And now she finds she*

161

can't read the paper in there, or perhaps she has decided to surprise me. Naturally she would learn the fundamentals of the game, when it is played in the inn parlor every night. (But he knew that she had not been deceiving him.) Then he saw that this new move of the queen's was in fact a clever attack, into which he could play and lose.

And then the guns around Kostrzyn, which had been silent since the early hours of the morning, began to boom again. Three times Lame Hans's hand stretched out to touch his king and make the move that would render it quite impossible for him to escape the queen, and three times it drew back. "You have five minutes in which to move," Doctor Eckardt said. "I will tell you when only thirty seconds remain, and count the last five."

The machine was built to play chess, thought Lame Hans. *Long ago, and they were warlocks in those days. Could it be that Gretchen, in kicking about . . . ?*

Some motion in the sky made him raise his eyes, looking above the board and over the top of the machine itself. An artillery observation balloon (gray-black, a German balloon then) was outlined against the blue sky. He thought of himself sitting in a dingy little shop full of tobacco all day long, and no one to play chess with—no one he could not checkmate easily.

He moved a pawn, and the black bishop slipped out of the king's row to tighten the net.

If he won, they would have to pay him. Heitzmann would think everything had gone according to plan, and Professor Baumeister, surely, would hire no assassins. He launched his counterattack: the real attack at the left side of the board, with a false one down the center. Professor Baumeister came to stand beside him, and Doctor Eckardt warned him not to distract the player. There had been seven more than fourteen moves—and there was a trap behind the trap.

He took the black queen's knight and lost a pawn. He was sweating in the heat, wiping his brow with his sleeve between moves.

A black rook, squat in its iron sandbags, advanced three squares, and he heard the crowd cheer. "That is mate, Herr Zimmer," Doctor Eckardt announced. He saw the look of relief on Professor Baumeister's face, and knew that his own was blank. Then over the cheering someone shouted: *"Cheat! Cheat!"* Gray-black pillbox police caps were forcing their way through the hats and parasols of the spectators.

"There is a man in there! There is someone inside!" It was too clear and too loud—a showman's voice. A tall stranger was standing on the topmost bench waving Heitzmann's sweat-stained velvet hat.

A policeman asked: "The machine opens, does it not, Herr Professor? Open it quickly before there is a riot."

Professor Baumeister said, "I don't know how."

"It looks simple enough," declared the other police-man, and he began to unfasten the catches, wrapping his hand in his handkerchief to protect it from the heat of the brass. "Wait!" ordered Professor Baumeister, but neither one waited; the first policeman went to the aid of the other, and together they lifted away one side of the machine and let it fall against the railing. The movable circuit card had not been allowed to swing back into place, and Gretchen's plump, naked legs pro-truded from the cavity beneath the chessboard. The first policeman seized them by the ankles and pulled her out until her half-open eyes stared at the bright sky. Doctor Eckardt bent over her and flexed her left arm at the elbow. "Rigor is beginning," he said. "She died of the heat, undoubtedly."

163

Lame Hans threw himself on her body weeping.

Such is the story of Lame Hans. The captain of police, in his kindness, has allowed me to push the machine to a position which permits Hans to reach the board through the bars of his cell, and he plays chess there all day long, moving first his own white pieces and then the black ones of the machine, and always losing. Sometimes when he is not quick enough to move the black queen, I see her begin to rock and to slide herself, and the dials and the console lights to glow with impatience; and then Hans must reach out and take her to her new position at once. Do you not think that this is sad for Lame Hans? I have heard that many who have been twisted by the old wars have these psychokinetic abilities without knowing it; and Professor Baumeister, who is in the cell next to his, says that someday a technology may be founded on them.

There's no accounting for fads . . . or is there? What about the sudden popularity of books like **A Grammar of the Tibetan Language** and **Tectonic Geology and the Coming Fifth Ice Age,** both of which became overnight bestsellers in dirty-book stores around the world? Surely there must be a sensible explanation for this, and we can trust R. A. Lafferty to figure it out. Of course, it depends on what we mean by "sensible."

R. A. Lafferty is the most individualistic writer in science fiction; his short-story collections include **Nine Hundred Grandmothers, Strange Doings** and **Does Anyone Else Have Something Further To Add?**

BRAIN FEVER SEASON

R. A. Lafferty

1

"Here's a puzzler," said Barnaby Sheen. "One of the hottest new items in the porno stores, not only in this country but worldwide also, is *A Grammar of the Tibetan Language* by A. Csoma de Koeroes. Odd name that! Does anybody know what he is? There are hasty translations of the grammar into a dozen languages within the last thirty-six hours (things go very fast in the porno field). Does anybody know why the heavy-breathing, rheumy-eyed passion boys and girls should have this sudden interest in a Tibetan grammar?"

"It is funny," said Doctor George Drakos, "and I

sure cannot see any reason for it. There's some sort of symbolism or transference, I suppose."

"As I recall it, Koeroes' book was printed in Calcutta in 1834," Cris Benedetti said. "If there is a venereal element in it, it should have surfaced long ago. Several generations of British civil servants studied it. But I don't believe it ranks among the great grammars, even for Tibetan."

"Austro!" Barnaby Sheen called loudly. And then there was a carrying whisper from the inner or omygosh room: "Carrock, oh, oh, what now?" Austro had learned to whisper most imperfectly (his people were unacquainted with the thing), and his whispers weren't quiet ones.

We always said that if anything should go wrong anywhere in the world, Barnaby Sheen would immediately suspect young Austro of having a hairy thumb in it. "Yes, and I'd be right to suspect him," Barnaby would always maintain. "He *would* have a hairy thumb in it, no matter what it was."

"Austro!" Barnaby called still more loudly.

"Carrock! I just *got* to go down to the laboratory, Mr. Sheen," Austro jabbered as he came from the inner room and made for the stairs down to the front door. "Whatever you want, it has to wait. I got to get down there right now."

"Don't tell me I have to wait, boy," Barnaby said. "It's eleven at night. The lab has been closed for hours. Whatever it is that *you* want will wait till tomorrow, Austro. Come here and talk."

"No, no, I got a hot smart idea," Austro protested. "I got to go to the lab and get it down on stone right now. We can't take chances on me forgetting it."

"You have stone tablets here, Austro," Barnaby said. "You've been hammering and chiseling on them in the omygosh room all evening. You can cut a hot idea into any of the stones so you'll remember it. You never forget anything anyhow. Roy Mega says that you never learned the trick of forgetting, and he hasn't been able to teach you. That's why you have such a cluttered mind. Austro, what do you know about the Tibetan language?"

"Carrock, it's tone-talk, a little bit like we talk at home. It's singsong stuff, but I never learned it very well. Oh Mr. Sheen, I got to go right now!"

"Austro, do you know why an obscure Tibetan grammar should suddenly become a hot item in the porno stores?"

"Mr. Sheen, you know I'm not old enough to go into the porno stores."

"No, but you're old enough to avoid a direct answer to a straight question. Austro, if this little puzzler were handed to you, what first step would you take toward finding the answer?"

"Carrock, I'd triangulate in on it. I'd find where the puzzler originated and where it spread from. Oh, oh, oh, why don't I learn to swallow my tongue? Why do you ask me questions? I'm just a twelve-year-old kid. Got to go right now!" And Austro ran down the stairs and out of the house.

Barnaby Sheen phoned Roy Mega at his mysterious number at his mysterious room. Nobody was sure where Roy Mega lived, but Barnaby Sheen believed that the young man had a room rigged up in that very house. Barnaby's was a big and junky house (most persons know how many rooms there are in their houses and where they are, but not Barnaby), and Roy had a cavalier way with space, and with telephones. Barnaby was sure that he was paying the phone bill on Roy's mysterious phone at least.

"Roy!" Barnaby barked into the phone. "Do you

know why an obscure Tibetan grammar should suddenly become a hot item in the porno stores?"

"Do you believe me the sort of young man who goes to the porno stores?" Roy asked out of the phone. "I'm hurt. Besides, it isn't obscure any longer. Got to hang up now. Got to go down to the lab and work on a hot idea."

"Hold it, Roy, hold it!" Barnaby ordered. "Tell me just exactly what you and Austro have been working on in the lab for the last three days. I do pay the bills there. You do work for me. I have the right to know what you're doing."

"Oh, we've been working on the relationship of shape to smell to season, Mr. Sheen. And especially on the relation of subliminal shape to subliminal smell to forgotten season. Sorry. Got to go now."

"Hold it, Roy!" Barnaby pressured. "Can there be a subliminal shape? Or a subliminal smell?"

"Oh, sure. We make them all the time. You think that things down underneath don't have any shape? Or that they don't have any smell? Keep reading the journals and you'll find out about our stuff. We really can't take time to inform every jasper of all the smart things that we're doing."

"Roy, if you were asked to solve the problem of Tibetan grammars suddenly becoming hot items in porno stores all over the world, where would you start?"

"I'd start the same place as with any other problem. I'd find out where *it* starts. Then it's easier to find out what it means. I'd triangulate in on it and find out who created the situation and started the problem to rolling around the world. Oh, oh, oh, I've got to invent an automatic guardian for myself! We hadn't decided what we wanted to do with it yet. Why do I say things? Got to go now! Got to go down to the lab for one of those brilliant sessions."

168

"Hold it, Roy! You're out of order," Barnaby crackled. "Now I—"

"The person is out of order. This is a recording," came over the phone. And already there were rapid Roy Mega footfalls going down a back stairway of the house. Wherever Roy's mysterious room was, it was toward the back of the house somewhere.

"I will bet that triangulation shows the origin of the puzzler to be right here in our own city, Barnaby," Doctor George Drakos said cheerfully.

"I will bet it shows that the origin is in your own lab building," Harry O'Donovan said.

"I will bet it shows the origin to be in the noggins of Austro and Roy Mega," Cris Benedetti said, "in those two orbs that beat as one."

"Why should such things be done in my own tents, and I have not done them?" Barnaby demanded in his scriptural boom. "That would be near treachery."

Roy Mega was a young man of the species Genius who worked for Barnaby Sheen at his lab. He was from a downtown family. Austro was a still younger man of the species Australopithecus who also worked for Barnaby in his house and at his lab. He was from the Guna Slopes in Africa.

And this was really an interesting puzzle. Well, why do *you* think that the Tibetan grammars had become just about the hottest items worldwide in the porno stores? And why do you think that other items almost as strange had become almost as hot?

For, by the next morning (the third morning that the new tendencies had been noticed), there were very many of the sudden and learned items going hot guns in the porno stores. These were mostly writings and clips and tapes and presentations of an apparent non-porno sort. Many of them clearly fell into the hot-brain

169

classification. And there was a double puzzle connected with all the things.

First: not one of the porno owners or operators around town knew how he had happened to order, for instance, a hundred and twenty copies of Masterman's *Tectonic Geology and the Coming Fifth Ice Age,* nor even how he knew there was such a book to order. And second: nobody knew why the habitual customers of the porno stores should buy and devour such a book so eagerly, so hotly, and with such absolute mental and personal comprehension of it. For the porno folks *did* comprehend the new material: and some of it would be thought difficult.

Yeah, and then there was the second part of the first puzzle: none of the publishers or manufacturers knew how he had arranged to have so many copies of the items available at that time. They had published a hundredfold above the expected, and they were being snapped up at a hundredfold above the expected.

Why, just consider some of the items. There were old and erudite works by Tobias Dantzig and Erwin Panofsky and Basil Wiley and Samuel Noah Kramer and J. Huizinga and Bertrand Flornoy and Karl Mannheim and Albert Einstein and Hans Vaihinger. Until the last two days or so one didn't find such things in the porno stores at all. They simply hadn't been sold anywhere by the tens of thousands every day before, and they hadn't been available in such volume till some strange anticipatory impulse had moved the publishers and manufacturers to unusual production.

There were young and pulsating works by Hildebrand Muldoon, Peter Zielinski, Robin Popper, Martin Gander, Virgil Whitecrow, Titus Hornwhanger, Albert Cotton. It was a boom in snappingly live information, but why was it flowering in the sleazy soil and not in proper pots?

By noon of the third day, there was a flood of second-generation or feedback works, most of them from the new Porno Ancilla Press, which had four thousand titles (of incomparable brilliance) stocked and selling before it was forty-eight hours old. Yes, things had always moved very fast in the porno field, but now they were moving in new directions.

The wonder was not in the ability of the porno people to meet and master such works of cosmology and extratemporal history and nonorganic psychology and shape-and-perspective chemistry and chthonic electricity. All peoples have about the same mental and personal ability and about the same quantity of power and apperception. The wonder was that the porno people, having for a long time devoted themselves to a different complex of things, should now come with such hot interest to the fields of dynamic information and implementation, to the kinetically constructed scientific-scholastic-innovative fields.

And then there were the newly oriented porno people themselves, the hot-brained generation, the nation in a hurry, the scorchy harvest. They were in such rapid movement that even their oddities were a high-speed color blur. One of them came a-touring into Barnaby Sheen's house that third noon.

"Who turned me on, odd fish?" this visitor asked as he came in on nervous but exuberant fox feet, with two dozen books in his arms and one opened in his left hand. "I was in Singapore, our mother city, the porno capital of the world, and it hit me there. 'Why haven't you Emanuel Visconti's *Costive Cosmologies Freed?* I howled at a storekeeper. 'How will I ever live another moment without it? I'm hot for it, man! I have to have it right now,' I said. And I never in all my life had heard of Visconti before. 'I hope we'll have it in a very few hours,' the porno man said. 'I'm mighty hot for it

171

myself, and getting hotter. Oh, there must be some way to speed it up!' 'A few hours!' I exploded at him. 'I can't wait a few hours. Don't you know when the time of a thing has arrived? What are you doing to get copies?' 'I've just been talking to Visconti,' the man said. 'He is in Istanbul, and he had begun it half an hour before I called. It'll take him fifteen to eighteen hours to do it, he says, and it will take several hours for printing and world distribution. It will be twenty hours yet. Here's two-dozen red-hot items that may tide you over.' 'What do you mean it will take him fifteen or eighteen hours to do it?' I demanded, panting hard. 'Oh, the work hasn't been written yet,' the porno proprietor said, 'but Visconti began it just as soon as the idea struck him.' Something is happening fast, Sheeny. It's happening in half of the world."

The man was speed-reading books as he talked. He threw one over his shoulder now and opened another.

"I see," said Barnaby Sheen. But he didn't see it at all clearly.

"But where did the happening begin?" asked the little foxy man. "I always like to be in the middle of a happening. I check the origin to very near this place, to be very near to you. I even get the cryptic message 'It's the sons of Sheeny.' I got that while I was riding Polynesian Airlines here. Who are the Sons of Sheeny, Sheeny?"

"I don't know, but I suspect," Barnaby said.

"I check it to near you, but I sure do not check it to you," the nervous and ardent man said. "Man, you're not on fire for it at all! You're not even alive to the new fever, and everything shows that you're in the middle of it. I'm Gippo Sharpface, by the way, and you, Sheeny, are Mr. Nobody himself."

"Did you locate this place by triangulation in on an influence?" Barnaby asked.

172

"Almost that. I'd realized since about midnight last night that the process would have to be distorted triangulation, since the phenomenon wasn't truly worldwide. But it's about the same thing. I located the center of the influence, and I found that the center was empty. The center is yourself. Can you tell me what is wrong, Sheeny?"

Gippo Sharpface was all this time speed-reading books and tossing them over his shoulder behind him like banana skins.

"I guess nothing is wrong," Barnaby said, "but I thought that the phenomenon *was* worldwide. It's of simultaneous appearance and development in Shanghai and Moscow and Istanbul and Stockholm and London and Cairo and New York and Toronto and Mexico City and Honolulu and Ponca City, Oklahoma. Just look at the charts that I have. Say, Gippo, how did a porno operator in Shanghai know where to phone Emanuel Visconti? He was completely unknown till yesterday, wasn't he?"

"Sheeny Sheen, those places you name don't make the world. Where is Capetown? Where is Sydney? Where are Buenos Aires and Rio? Why were things so unclear in Singapore, the porno capital of the world? No, there wasn't any rational way for the porno proprietor or myself or a million other people ever to have heard of Visconti. He had hardly heard of himself. There isn't any rational explanation for any of the hot instincts. But Emanuel Visconti was one of the hot instincts for a while. Not near as much today as yesterday, of course."

"The tendencies are only in the northern half of the world, are they, Gippo?" Barnaby asked. "That's interesting. And the emanating center is around here? Your triangulation shows that this is the center of it all?"

"Old Sheeny Nothing-Man, Not-With-It-Man, this

can't be the center of anything. What's that concrete-block building about fifty yards over there?"

"That's my laboratory. And the only persons working there lately are two lucky-brained young men. Sometimes I say that they comprise the left lobe of my own brain."

"Are they sometimes called the Sons of Sheeny?" Gippo demanded excitedly.

"Only by yourself," Barnaby said, "but nobody else could be called that at all. They're the two heads that beat as one. They're the hairy thumb and the smooth thumb in every bowl of stew. I suspected that they were involved."

"Yes, that's the emanating center, Sheen," Gippo said as he tossed another finished book over his shoulder. "That's the turned-on place. Could you have a cashier's check for a million dollars drawn up within twenty minutes or so? It will take at least that much for first ante if we're going to get in on this boom."

"Do you want to be turned off again, Gippo?" Barnaby asked. "Oh, I suppose I could have the money in one form or another within fifteen or twenty minutes."

"No, I don't want to be turned off again, Sheen, not while this season is running. I want a bucket. It's raining the queerest and hottest fish ever seen, and I have an overpowering lust for them. I want my passions fulfilled, and at the same time I want them to continue burning, and I want to make a good thing out of the hot rain while it is going on. Then I will have to find out where the next hot brain-rain or whatever will fall." At a jittery fox trot, Gippo Sharpface went down to the laboratory building, tossing books over his shoulder as he finished them.

Barnaby Sheen called several of us on the hot line that Roy Mega had rigged for him. We all agreed that a pleasantly hot sort of spring fever was going through everybody. We thought that it was an information-and-invention sort of fever and we didn't understand how it fit into the porno context, except for the sheer lust there might be in the new racking and sacking of knowledge. While we were on the hot line, Barnaby said that Austro had just come with a personal check of Barnaby's to be signed, a check for a million dollars. And Barnaby said that he was signing it with chisel and graver.

A Barnaby Sheen personal check would have been hard to forge, since Austro made them for him out of thin slate-stone. Nobody could imitate Austro's rock-engraving work. And nobody could imitate Barnaby's signature when he cut it into slate-stone with a square-blade tapered graver.

"That's more than I usually put into a thing on a hunch," Barnaby said. "Now I have crossed the Rubicon in this, or at least I have crossed Joe Creek."

But Barnaby needn't have worried. Within another thirty-six hours, he had put so much money into hot-information projects as to make that first ante of no great importance, whether he lost it or got it back.

Say, it was a bonfire of rampant mentality and discovery that took over the northern half of the world in the days that followed. Two weeks of that splendid and frightening spring fever brought more achievement than had the hundred-year-long fever that had once run through Athens, than the hundred-year-long fever that had once run through Florence. Besides, those older fevers had run off in all directions, but the present new-old burning was focused on knowledge and on sharp and swinging science. The focus of it was the main thing. There were few side runnels to it that were not concerned with knowledge. It was an ordered

175

and intense flooding of Hot Brain River. Every day brought new and generating lightning, like the flash that had opened up the new world, like the flash that had opened up the Copernican cosmos, like the flash that had opened up the atom. And the glorious explosion of knowledge was accepted and effected at once. What did it matter that the cargo had first been freighted in by grubby hands and grubby minds? The beneficent explosion was real now. The thing had gone on for nearly three weeks, and the world would never be the same as it had been before. The technology hadn't had a chance to follow up on all the breakthroughs, but that chance would come as soon as things had cooled off enough so that they might be touched. Or "I think it will catch up in a little bit different sort of season a little bit later in the year," Roy Mega said. What sort of talk was that?

Did anybody really understand what was happening? No, not completely, for it was happening exponentially. Well, was anybody finding a way to take advantage of what was happening? Oh, there were a few hundred of the sharpfaces who were. They found new sorts of buckets and bags and bushels to take portions of that post-material harvest. Here was treasure that would burn the fingers off you, and yet it could be handled by the handlers.

There were some who gathered the aromatic smoke and the tilt-spectrumed sunlight into coffers. (The stuff that had once been called knowledge had been raised by several powers, so it was not quite the same stuff it had been before.) There were some who raked and compressed the bright brainstorms into bales. There were the manipulating few who had the touch to garner intangibles and to label them "Special Commodity." There were several score of persons who could price and predict the tendencies of this commodity-market conflagration of ideas.

Gippo Sharpface did a little bit of the garnering and the prediction-calculating. Barnaby Sheen did a little of it, and he also seemed to own the results of others who were doing it. He said that, for quite a while there, he was making a million dollars an hour out of the fever. Some of the old-time porno operators were able to hang in there for a while, and some of the soft-stuff industrialists and foundation people did it. And new people who had been in the hot-brain business for only two or three weeks were now running ellipses around the world.

"Do you know for certain what day the season will end, Sheeny?" Gippo asked one day.

"Why should it ever end?"

"Oh, you don't understand the times and seasons, Sheen? How do you get along as well as you do? Austro says that it will end the day after the hot-brain full moon."

2

Austro could probably have explained the theory of it a little bit. He couldn't do it very well in words, but he could do it by symbols cut in his rock tablets. He explained pretty well even with words, but everybody was always too busy to listen.

"We used to set the seasons of the world from two locations," Austro said once. "One of these regions was the Guna Slopes, and the other was the Malawi Shores, the first about ten degrees north and the second about ten degrees south of the equator. And also, we were the ones who had set up the equator, but that's a different account. There were certain tricks with shape stuff and smell stuff that we used to get the seasons started, but

177

all of it was remember-and-reminder jog. It still is. People really feel when it's time for one season or another, but now-a-aeons they get busy and they don't feel it strongly enough."

"Quit the quacking and get busy, Austro," Barnaby Sheen ordered. "Start divining what's going to be a hot property tomorrow and where he can be found. You're good at that, but you're no good at the quacking and clacking."

"There's a lot to be said for the etiological aspect of the epochon," Austro said a minute later when Barnaby had gone elsewhere, "and their plastinx category apozemiosis, not to mention the helical reinforcement of the phengaric base, considering the former duration of the etos itself. Now, if we keep fifteen points firmly in mind—"

"Why all the Sunday words, Austro?" I asked him.

"Carrock, I'm trying to shake my ape-boy image," he said. "People think that all I can say is 'carrock.' Well, the hot-brain season is one of the seasons that the people have been too busy to remember. Of course we always remembered it back home, and we always had the hottest brains of anyone in the world. But we felt the other people dragging their feet, or dragging their lobes on it, and this slowed us down, since all people are a corporation. Ah, George, the hottest property tomorrow will be a Simon McCloy of Olathe, Kansas, in this very nation. This young man has just this minute broken his pool cue in total frustration, and if he can get hold of pencil and paper he will jot down a mass of the most astonishing mathematical tables ever. These will be revolutionary, in the manner of revolving or rotating vectors, but far beyond. They'll have a sort of tilt-spin to them. The number of the pool hall is 1-913-PH 99199."

"Got it, Austro," said Doctor George Drakos, who

178

was sort of a correlator of talent. "Table-tilting and mathematics belong together in hot-brain season. Now quit the jabber and stay with the divining stuff."

(Barnaby Sheen had drafted us all to work at his lab and in his sprawling house, running around with buckets to catch the hot-brain rain.)

"Back home we couldn't send the hints strong enough to overcome the indifference of the world-scattered peoples," Austro was saying. "We were not able to recall them to the duties and pleasures of the ordained seasons. The only electricity we had was the difference in potential between flint-stone and chert-stone. Here we can broadcast the hints with a real zing. And the people the zing hit first were the jaded-brained pornos who were always howling for faster and newer zings. But it's hit everybody now. If they all find that they like it, I bet they come easier to it next year."

"Get out of the way, Austro," Cris Benedetti shouted. "Why don't you come up with something new for the family-plan centers?"

Barnaby Sheen, in just two days' time, had set up nine thousand Family-Plan Hot-Brain Parlors to handle the brainster boom. The boom had long since outgrown the porno stores and it was a communal thing all the way. Brains called to brains and they made scorchy music together. In the country, the people gathered in the dingles and dells for their communal-knowledge oestrus or rut; but in the towns the Hot-Brain Parlors of Barnaby Sheen filled a need.

"Can't you move faster, Austro?" Harry O'Donovan was hollering. We all tried to get as much out of Austro as we could. He had talents, but they were lazy talents.

"How can I move faster, Harry? I'm only a twelve-year-old kid," Austro protested.

"The hot-brain season is really a kid thing," Austro
179

continued when Harry O'Donovan was off hollering somewhere else, "but I don't think anyone gets too old to enjoy it. It's real fun to be smart in the smart season. One time down in the Gunas we went in for shooting stars in the hot-brain season. We really shot them out. I mean it. That was only a few thousand years ago. Guys are still puzzled about all those old novas that seemed to happen at the same time. That was about as high going as anybody ever went, even in hot-brain season. Who's got hot enough brains to do it now?"

"Get out of the way, Austro," Gippo Sharpface barked. "You can chatter when hot-hammock season gets here. That's what it's for."

Roy Mega could have explained the theory of it a little bit, if anyone had had the time to listen to him.

"Conveying subliminal shapes electronically was easy enough," Roy was saying, "and of course shape is a big part of the stimulus. But our biggest difficulty was conveying subliminal smells at electronic speeds to electronic distances. Smells are essential to it. We had to hype ourselves up and then wait for the hot-brain season to hit the two of us. That's the reason that the season in general was really almost nine hours late. We weren't smart enough to do it on time. It took us nine hours to get smart enough, and then to make and transmit the jog-keys to remind the peoples of the world that a new hot season was here. But after we were hit by the smarts we could work out anything."

"But just what is it, Roy?" I asked him. I had the idea now that everybody except myself knew what was going on.

"Why, it's only the seasons of the world and of the world's people," Roy Mega said. "It's the old oestrus and the rutting. People are supposed to have their hot and bright seasons, first for one thing, then for another.

180

But when people started to live under roofs they lost part of their feeling for the seasons. Then they said that they would stay hot on everything all the year around, and they lost another part of it. They really lost the edge of it then. They barely managed to stay lukewarm on everything. And then they lost even that. Every day is a holiday when the hot seasons are observed, and things really get generated."

"Why is the brain-bust going on in only the northern hemisphere, Roy?" I asked.

"Because the brain-bust is a natural season, and the natural seasons are reversed down there. They're having their own rut down south right now, but you'd hardly believe it if I told you what it was. It's one of the forgotten things that sure hadn't ought to be forgotten."

"How long will the hot-brain season last here?" I asked him.

"Oh, till the hot-brain full moon. You'll feel it when the season leaves you. And you'll feel a little bit empty. Yeah, for about a minute. Then the next rut season will hit you and you'll be overtaken by something just as strong as hot brains, and entirely different."

"Get out of the way, Mega and Laff!" Barnaby Sheen was bellowing. "Why do I pay starvation wages around here? Just to hear you guys jabber?"

"Is anybody taking care of it Down South?" I asked Austro when next the straw bosses were busy elsewhere.

"Sure, a cousin of mine is doing it down there," he said. "This cousin was raised on the Malawi Shores, and then he was shanghaied to Rio as a kid. Now he's teamed up with a cross-eyed carioca youngster who's kind of like Roy Mega. They're pretty good at it down there, almost as good at it as Roy and I are."

"How many hot seasons are there in the year, Austro?" I asked him.

"Get out of the way, Austro and Laff!" Benedetti was howling. "There's work to do."

Well, it was fun. Every day, though we worked long hours, was really a holiday. It's fun to be smart. And the smarter you are, the more fun it is. Those who deny this are those who've never had any really smart days in their lives. It's top fun when the whole world is smart, or the top half of it anyhow. There's really excitement in learning everything, everything, and then exploding it into bigger and bigger versions of itself. It's like doubling your life's knowledge every day, and then doubling it again the next day. It's like—

(—time is compressed here, and the brain days are all run together. There is too much of it for analysis, though analysis of everything else is part of the brain days. The pleasure is still too near to be put into words, and they say that the hot-brain jag will be even better next year.)

"There's a new corporation trying to buy me out," Barnaby Sheen said one evening. "The corporation is made up of the second, third, and fourth biggest people in the hot-brain cash-in complex. But I'm still number one. Why should I sell?"

"Sell before the sun goes down, Sheeny," Gippo Sharpface told him. "And then pull a few millions off the roll for us your faithful and seasonable minions."

"But the thing is getting bigger and bigger," Barnaby puffed.

"And tonight is hot-brain full moon," Austro said. "Oh sure, it'll be back again next year. Well, sell now and you will have the means to handle it next year any way you want to. Sell it, carrock!"

"At a certain hour we will send out a new shape and a new smell and a new sound," said Roy Mega. "And these things will trigger a new hot season."

"Ah, yeah, I hear the new sound now," Barnaby said. "It's the sound that the merry-go-round makes just before it breaks down."

Barnaby Sheen had to hurry, but he did manage to sell his hot-brain empire before the sun went down.

3

Barnaby Sheen was stamping out a multitude of burning cigar butts. Or else he was dancing some funny dance in the early morning. I had never seen him dance before, but he wasn't bad.

"Loppity, Goppity, Gippity, Gopes—I'm a little kid from the Guna Slopes," Austro was singing with the ringing upper half of his voice, and he was filling the air with rock dust as he cut the same immortal galloping words into a rock slab. At that moment, Austro was the hottest poet in the world.

Gippo Sharpface, wearing outsized dark glasses, was facing directly into the bright morning sun, and he was painting it: a burningly brilliant orb, which was wearing outsized dark glasses. Gippo was doing absolutely new things with color, burning things, foxfire things. Gippo, at that moment, was the finest artist that the world has seen for the last twenty thousand years.

Doctor George Drakos was sitting on a little stool. He was holding a surgeon's bone-saw. He had put a double bend into it, and he was striking it with a bone-chiseler's hammer. And you wouldn't believe the music he was making. George Drakos, at that moment, was the finest musical-saw player the world had ever seen.

Cris Benedetti was wearing a toga, and he had

pieces of laurel looped around his ears. He was declaiming drama. It wasn't old Shakespearean drama or any such thing. It was old-new Cris Benedetti drama. It was ringing and riming and eloquent like real hot-art season drama. It moved one to passion and pleasure. Evoked forms crowded the golden morning, and the fine voice of Cris called out real response. At that moment, Cris Benedetti was the finest dramatic declaimer in the world.

Harry O'Donovan was sculpturing something in lucite and chrome. It was primordial form made out of the primordial elements of fire and ice. It was almost the secret of life itself, it was almost the shape of destiny. It was probably good.

And the voice of Mary Mondo the ghost girl was doing cantatas and those other flutey songs. And she *was* good. She had probably always been in accord with the hot seasons.

Roy Mega was producing some sort of delta-secondary music by manipulation of split-frequency circuits. Ah well, nobody had ever done quite that thing before, and the first of everything is always good by definition.

"The hot-art season, huh!" Barnaby Sheen commented, still doing his cigar-butt stomp-out dance. "Did you guys know that it would be the next season? There ought to be a way to make a good thing out of it. Austro, do you know who will be the hottest art property in the world by midmorning?"

"Carrock, I know, I won't tell," Austro caroled. "Moppity, Loppity, Lippity, Moan—Let it alone, man, let it alone!" Austro sure made the rock dust fly when he was graving his verses on stone and singing his own accompaniment to chisel and graver.

"For the sanctification of your soul, don't squeeze every season, Sheeny," great artist Gippo Sharpface said. "Ah, what nobility and blaze of color! I frighten

184

myself with my own genius. But let this one go, Sheen."

"What, You the Fox say that? But I've the feeling you're right. I think I'll go write me a thundering epic drama. It will begin with the Chorus of May Dancers doing a stunning dance sort of like the one I've been doing. Say, are the seasons inexorable under the revised system? Their returning is a freedom-of-expression thing, of course, but must we follow just one sequence in them? We should have a choice in this too."

"There's another world down under," Roy Mega said.

"What follows the hot-art season here?" Gippo Sharpface asked. And the sun in his painting was brighter than the sun in the sky.

"The hot-rock season will come next," Austro told us. "That's when the people have a fever for building huge structures out of every material, but rock is still prince of materials. Did you know that the Great Pyramid was built in a single hot-rock season?"

"Does anyone know what is playing down under now?" Harry O'Donovan asked.

"It's the hot-love season just starting there," Roy Mega said. "Some people believe that it was the original oestrus, the first hot wave."

Gippo Sharpface made a sudden noise. Then he effected one more burning splotch on his splendid painting. "Gad, what genius!" he cried in humble admiration, "but the very greatest things, by their nature, must be left unfinished." He signed the unfinished sun painting "Fire Fox."

"I'm off, fellows," he said then. "Hot love was always my first love. I can pick up the hot-art season again once or even twice a year. And I'll catch the hot-brain season again, either down there or back here again next spring. But something is calling me down there right now. Anyone else for Rio? Austro?"

"No, no. I'm scared of that stuff," the greatest rock-graving poet in the world refused it. "Maybe next year. I'm at the bashful stage now. Carrock, I'm only a twelve-year-old kid."

"I'm with you, Gippo," Harry O'Donovan said, and he left his sculptured lucite and chrome that was almost the secret of life itself.

"In just three more moons it'll be hot-love season here, fellows," Roy Mega said reasonably. But Gippo and Harry were already gone.

"Gippity, Goppity, Goopity, Gouth—Gippo and Harry are fire-tailing South," Austro sang and chiseled his great folk poem.

It's wonderful to hear the greatest poet of an age in action.

The idea of time travel is so appealing that it's become a standard plot device in science fiction, despite the fact that by all standards of logic it's clearly impossible: visiting the past would violate the cause-and-effect basis of scientific thinking. But perhaps it **would** be possible for future chrononauts to observe the past by inhabiting the minds of selected people . . . and what historian in any field could resist such an opportunity? Especially the chance to share with Beethoven the composition of his greatest work, the Ninth Symphony?

Carter Scholz, who builds from this idea a dramatic tale of the anomalies of creation, is a graduate of the Clarion SF Writers' Workshops whose previous stories have appeared in **Orbit, Alternities, Clarion IV** and **Output.**

THE NINTH SYMPHONY OF LUDWIG VAN BEETHOVEN AND OTHER LOST SONGS

Carter Scholz

1

When a man's halfway to his death, he knows. The bones shift, the organs settle, the blood ticks out a quiet warning: time's half gone, look around, what've you done, what are you *going* to do? Every day we meet reminders of our mortality and dismiss them, uneasily ignore, turn our faces from the grave. But at that halfway mark, ignorance is impossible; a man thinks, My God, I'm thirty-five, I'm forty, and the years are relentless, I'll never be thirty or twenty or fifteen again—and was I ever? Did I ever look around, feel, really *know* eighteen or twenty-four or any of my ages? Did I make the most of them?

Charles Largens woke one morning and found himself there. He thought, I'm thirty-five years old and I won't live past seventy. My bones tell me in language I can't rebuff. Half my life is gone, and oh Lord, where?

The early years had gone into two sonatas, an unfinished symphony, a mass, an incomplete song cycle. Those were good years, good work. But since then his time had gone into research, criticism; it had been made solid, not in sounds but in vast stacks of paper, dreary essays and analyses. He did not enjoy it, and often the stuff had no meaning for him, but it took his time nonetheless. It had taken half his life.

In his voicetyper was an unfinished essay on Buxtehude; he had abandoned it last night when the fugues and inventions piled up in a baroque tangle and he could make no more sense of them. Notes had swarmed past his eyes like flies on a five-staved racetrack, the precise ordered counterpoint a frightening miniature of his own boxed and formal life. He fell asleep with that image and woke to the sudden shock of being thirty-five. And he thought of Ludwig Van Beethoven, his avatar, the one constant source of solace in his life. He wanted to be Beethoven that morning, more than he ever had before.

Such a thing was not impossible. It was not easy to be Beethoven, of course. Like most of the Lincoln Center musicologists in the year 2016, he had been trying the greater part of his career for that distinction; and only now, after years of the lesser talents, the Couperins and Loeschorns and Bertinis, and atop that awful sense of waste and futility, did he feel ready to consider the Master.

But be honest: it was more than consideration; this morning he recognized it as an obsession. Bach and Chopin and Debussy and even old Buxtehude were fine in their places, but for him, Charles Largens, only one composer had all the balance, the power, the complete rightness that music ought to have; so as a pianist might dream of Carnegie (as he once had), or an artist of the Guggenheim, or a literary critic of *Finnegans Wake,* so Largens longed to base his lifework as musicologist on the works of Beethoven. More now; as Beethoven he might transcend the study of music, and attain the abstract itself. That was the dream that kept him going those years after his own music went dry, the dream that drove him to write essays on the preludes of Moskowski and bore himself to madness with Czerny just because he had been a student of the Master's; just because that particular essay might draw some attention, make someone cry, Hey! he's got it! and you could never tell what might attract the men with power, the men with the machines, so you did it all.

He wanted to be Beethoven, and these men could do that for him, with their machines.

The machines were windows into the past. Not doors, nor even a very clear sort of window; they more revealed the texture of the glass than the scene beyond, for what they did was transfer your consciousness into the mind of someone in the past.

After the historians found that subjective impressions of history were not very much more valuable than textbooks and records, the psychologists and scholars took over the vast banks of transfer equipment; they roamed and delved the past like archaeologists in a newly unearthed Greek library. Essays appeared psychoanalyzing Freud. The real reasons for the Emancipation Proclamation were revealed. The Shakespeare/Bacon myth was finally debunked. George Washington's real name came out. And it was inevitable that the artists, the writers, the musicians, in their mutual despair of ever taking art further than it had already gone in the barren year 2016, came forward eager to learn the inspirations for *Macbeth, Also Sprach Zarathustra, Waiting for Godot,* the Beethoven Ninth. To find out if El Greco was really astigmatic; to catch Hemingway's last thoughts as he triggered the shotgun; to study firsthand the mad genius of Van Gogh; to see the world as the great minds of history saw it. To put together in the sad flat year 2016 a world, piecemeal, from remnants of the past.

Time travel, of a sort; it was not real time travel, for that would have been magic, a kind of miracle, and there were no more miracles or magic in the world they had made. It was a world of norms and averages and no extremes, a world where everything had an explanation and a reason, where even this miraculous-seeming time travel could be expressed in hard clear terms, if you had the math. There were no paradoxes; the mind occupied seemed to have no awareness of its passengers. The passengers could only observe, could not touch the past. One might even jump back into one's own life and affect it not at all (aside perhaps from some slight *déjà vu).* Of course, the government kept the tightest of reins on the process; so only now, after ten years with the very elite Lincoln Center Research Group, did Charles Largens feel qualified to ask for Beethoven, to accept that last resort.

It was his essay on the inspirations of Buxtehude that drew the attention of H. Grueder, chairman of the board deciding past inhabitations. Largens had been studying the lesser talents for those ten years; he had even inhabited a few. And now his patience had paid its reward: word was out that Charles Largens was a man to watch, a man on the edge of success. And the only thing dulling his sense of triumph was that ineluctable, tender realization that he had never meant to be a musicologist. He had joined the Lincoln Center group as a pianist and composer; but the tenor of the times was research over performance, study before passion; and call it weakness, expediency, what you will, he had found himself more in the archives than in the practice rooms. After some years those quantitative changes became qualitative: he stopped even calling himself a composer; he was a musicologist (sharp Latin percussives), still a student of music, but now from the cold side: theory over practice, intellect over heart. As a boy he had dreamed of long polished grand pianos, warm and shining under bright spots, their keyboard mouths open and waiting, and beyond the stage's edge a blinding darkness filled with murmurs and the rustlings of programs, shirts, gowns. And ovations, storms of applause like all the warm summer showers that ever were, drenching him to a blissful numbness. But his life of composing was not that way; it was drab and hungry, and he wanted so desperately the color of a great composer's life. And what easier, directer way than the transfers? At first he told himself that his own work would profit from the contacts with past greats; but he knew it was a lie—he found that the contacts withered his own impulses. He was glutted, stuffed with music not his own. Several times in those years he had wanted to quit, get out, go back to composing—but the money was good, he was sometimes acclaimed for his critical insights as he had not been for his music, and he had a fear that perhaps he could not compose any more. And too, as his own music faded, there was the growing dream of Beethoven.

The morning that dream seemed ready to come real, the morning Grueder sent for him, he was met by George Santesson outside the conference room. The rest of the board was inside, waiting for him; the separate and personal greeting from Santesson was a surprise. The big man smiled broadly and wrung his hand with real warmth. "Nervous?" he whispered. Largens nodded.

"Don't worry, you'll make it. I read your essay. You'll do fine."

Largens felt warm. He fumbled for a way to extend the moment. "I feel as nervous as I did at my conservatory tryout."

Santesson smiled in appreciation. "You majored in composition, didn't you?"

"Yes. I see you've been doing research on me."

"One likes to know about one's future colleagues." With that, Santesson pushed open the thick leather-covered door and they entered. Largens' heart surged: Santesson was head of Beethoven Studies. Such confidence was heady stuff.

He seated himself at the far end of an oval table. Grueder congratulated him on his essay, shuffled through some notes, and finally asked the long-awaited question: Who? Who would it be next? Offering him his choice of composers for extended study, with full inhabitation rights. He had the strange feeling that Grueder already knew—Santesson certainly did—the feeling that this was all formality, that the decision was already made. He had for that second the feeling of a defendant watching the jury file back in.

He said Beethoven, and there was no surprise. Grueder nodded, made a notation on a schedule, a tiny precise scratching motion with his antique pen, and said he didn't see why not, and that Largens would be permitted a preliminary occupation during the composing of the first piano sonata, 1793, full rights pending approval of the results of that study. Was that acceptable?

Largens thanked everyone several times.

Santesson was on hand the next day, too, when Largens showed up at the transfer room with a head full of anticipations, and, stupidly, a notebook. He and Santesson laughed at that. Then the older man wished him luck and left him alone with the technicians.

They asked him a number of questions about his ancestry and mental health while they took an EEG and ran some machines of which he could see only the exposed backs, and finally they brought him a paper cup full of orange juice.

"What's this?" Largens asked.

"A hallucinogen. Very mild. It prepares you for the transfer."

"I never had to do this before."

"You were never trying to get into Beethoven's head before. He has a tremendous alpha potential. If you didn't drink this, it'd be like mismatching audio impedances; you'd never get across."

He was led into a thick-carpeted room more like a den than a laboratory: rich tapestry colors and subdued yellow lights instead of harsh fluorescents. Purposes of setting, he presumed. The only visible electronics were a stereo system and a tangle of multicolored wires that spilled from a wall socket into spaghetti patterns on the couch. The silence could be felt, like the pressure preceding a storm; behind the wall hangings there must have been acoustical tiles.

"Would you undress now, Mr. Largens?" someone said.

His clothes came off with more friction than usual, it seemed; his hearing seemed somehow bent, his vision slightly fragmented. They taped electrodes to him: cold metal gooseflesed his neck and arms, his groin, the small of his back, behind his ears. He felt the coldness spreading to cover his skin with hallucinatory foil. He heard a thunk and a quiet hissing as someone set a phono needle down. A tickling began behind his ears and Beethoven's first piano sonata began to play in his head

swimming in sounds that spiraled up around him, came together in his head and canceled gravity, he could feel billions of tiny soft points of velvet grow and lift him through the liquid sky with the first piano notes rising, pulsing colors on the horizon, and each note had a texture, this C like rough dark wood, that F a silky coldness, an A like a trapped bumblebee in his hands, and the music was no longer coming into him through his ears but was bursting out from within like a spontaneous song breaking free and sailing into a clear summer sky, apart from its source, apart from time, it carried Largens and he had no sense of going forward or going back or anything other than motion itself, of shutting his eyes and feeling the gone world whirl beneath him, he was a child flat back on a grassy plain, eyes clenched tight at the sky and fingers dug into fistfuls of earth and the whole world spinning and spinning and nothing but spinning, the motion, the vertigo, circles and currents, layers of moire confusion, oceans and waves rolling and rolling, the perpetual roll and flat scream of things that change and never change, moving not moving, the seasons that spin down a spiral of time, the ocean that crawls and rolls under its map-flat surface, the planets that turn and spin, each its own clock, the moving and complete motions of the instantaneous universe. He was moving through the first movement of the first piano sonata of the beginning of a long and turbulent life full of its own movements and motions, songs wound into a soul and waiting for release, steps to be taken through meadows and woods and narrow cobbled streets, wines to be tasted . . . and it all shifted and was moving him somewhere, the motion and the music becoming one and leading him into a life whose goal was their perfect union.

There was a darkness, and a light, as Largens opened his new eyes onto Vienna of 1794.

2

Cries and the beat of hooves and the rumble and clatter of wagons through mudpuddled streets reached him as he lurched to consciousness. The windows of the room leaned open to catch the afternoon rain-freshened air, and the sun struck rainbow brilliances off watery glass. The voices Largens heard could have been Beethoven's subconscious musings or the town's glad emergence after the storm. Beethoven went to the window and breathed deeply. Largens dizzied with the sights and sounds and smells of his dream come real, and he wept. He tried to put his hands to his face, and of course nothing happened. Foolish man, he fondly cursed himself, crying without eyes, expecting another man's body to express your joy. But if he was physically detached, the spiritual union was incredible. This was no fantasy; he *was* Beethoven, he could feel every ache and exultation of the composer's soul, and he had never before known what life could be like—! To have the world spread before you, to sense the forces of destiny shifting like banks of clouds or strata of earth—this was what it was to be great, to carry genius within you like a seed, a freight of potency. Very early in his own life Largens had felt the hints of this. In a way, his whole life had been an attempt to recapture that

195

lost greatness. And here, Beethoven: with no doubt of his own importance, even so young. As young as Largens had been when he entered the Center. The drab improbable world of the future, his past.

Beethoven's mind was warm and sparkling. It idled and hummed with life like a brook in late spring; thoughts mixed and swirled in currents of warm and cool. Beethoven was content simply to be in his new lodgings and to peer out the large crystal windows overlooking the street where movers struggled in with his belongings. The sweet force of this content washed Largens.

Largens reviewed the history of the moment: it was late in the year; Beethoven had just moved to Count Carl Lichnowsky's house in Vienna, Alserstrasse 45. Here he would earn a substantial salary for composing and performing, and form a rare lasting friendship with the Count. *Dem Fursten Carl von Lichnowsky gewidmet.* He remembered the words from the top of a piano sonata he had played when young.

Beethoven paced the room, brooding. He thought rapidly, in fragments of dialect. Words, sounds, gave shape to music, which he visualized rather than heard. Once visualized, he immediately orchestrated the phrase. Only occasionally did he go to the piano to play out a bar. At last he began to play a full piece, the second movement of his first piano sonata.

Largens waited. This movement had been written piecemeal years before, but there were other things in the composer's mind, and Largens could sense syntheses occurring between what was played and what was imagined. He watched the young fingers triphammer up and down arpeggios with a certain vicarious satisfaction, a remote pride. With two final flourished chords, the movement ended, and Largens' mind leaped to full attention.

Beethoven leaned over the keyboard, pondering. Then he lifted a quill, inked it, and began to write . . .

Hours later Largens awoke in Manhattan, screaming German curses. He blinked twice and settled foolishly back onto the couch as an attendant unwound wires, disconnected meters, and handed him his clothes. He stared at them as if they had changed color, or shrunk three sizes. He was acutely disoriented. A doctor standing near the door watched Largens and made notes on a flat glowing pad.

"I . . . he was having a tantrum," Largens explained. "He lost his temper at a mover for interrupting him. He . . ." His thoughts fluttered. He shook his head. "Why am I so woozy?"

The doctor said, "Could be the drug."

"But I've taken them before; I never felt like this. Are you sure it's nothing serious?"

The doctor regarded him coldly. "We are not *sure* of anything, Mr. Largens."

"Did I say something wrong?"

"Nothing. Not a thing. It's a little idiosyncrasy of mine that I snap at people for no reason at all."

"For what reason are you snapping at me?"

The doctor thumbed off his light-pen. "It's a little matter of responsibility, Mr. Largens. Of all the ways you could be spending this money—and for that matter, your time, though I suppose that's your business—this strikes me as the most wasteful and dangerous. If I had my way, you people wouldn't be mucking around in the past at all. We just don't know enough about it. But you've got your government lobbies, and people must have their novelties, so you're allowed to go. Let's leave it at that. But don't expect me to get too concerned over your dizziness."

"If you feel that way, why do you work here?"

The doctor paused, and had a look Largens knew: the hard, bitter look of a man who knows just how much of himself he has sold, and how cheaply. "I intend to start a free clinic with my salary from here." He clipped the pen in his pocket and walked out.

The attendant put away a handful of wires. "Don't mind him. Professional paranoia. Every week a different worry. This week it's something called a crosstalk effect."

"What's that?"

"Well, when you have a cable or a magnetic tape or a laser carrying more than one channel of information, there's always a certain amount of leakage between channels. If one channel's quiet you can hear the others coming through. That's crosstalk. The more channels, the worse it gets. So they're especially worried about guys like Beethoven; sometimes he has a dozen or more researchers in his head at once. They're worried about that."

"What, that Beethoven might overhear thoughts from the future?"

"Something like that."

"Oh, but that's absurd. Even if Beethoven heard anything, he'd never guess the source. He'd think it was . . ." Largens slowed.

"Inspiration. Intuition. You begin to see?"

Largens stood silent. He thought of Da Vinci's notebooks, the visions of Blake. For a second in the murmur of the air conditioning, he thought he could hear a dozen researchers from *his* future whispering in one corner of his mind.

"Oh, but after all . . ."

The attendant held up his hand. "I know, I know. I won't argue it. It's one of those damned paradoxes. Could be, couldn't be. That's why they're upset. Until they can *prove* any of it, there's nothing they can do. And how do you prove a paradox?"

So there were paradoxes, after all.

In the first piano sonata of Ludwig Van Beethoven, the influence of his tutor Josef Haydn is clearly felt. Haydn seems to guide the young composer's pen from time to time. But

In this, his first sonata, the young Beethoven first breaks from his classical antecedents. The second movement seems to be saying a last farewell to the "galant" age. Breaking from the strict regimen of Haydn's instruction,

The first sonata might be called a tribute to Haydn. The composer moves with great surety through these familiar

Here the young Beethoven's craftsmanship still shows sign of immaturity, as when the splendid A-flat major cantilena is prevented from fully developing by a clumsy

The second movement is not in sonata form, but is rather a rhapsody, laid out

Beethoven's originality

Yes, yes, but where did he get his ideas?

At six Santesson came in to wish him good-night. All day Largens had been working on his essay and it had gone nowhere. The older man read the desk at a glance, took in the litter of half-written pages, abandoned beginnings, and all that they meant—and gave

Largens a sympathetic nod. There must have been something near desperation in the young man's face, because Santesson paused as he was leaving, and motioned Largens to follow.

They went down the empty halls, the last ones in the building. They did not speak. They reached the transfer room and only then did Largens have an intimation of their purpose. Santesson fumbled a key from his pocket, slid the door open, and sealed it after them before turning on the lights.

The room stood empty and silent. Humming.

"Do you know how to use the equipment, Charles?"

"No."

For half an hour Santesson detailed the use of the machinery, scrupulously, completely, until Largens could have started it alone, sent himself on a retrogressive voyage—and at the end of it Santesson pressed a key into his hand. "In case you ever need to," he whispered. And left Largens alone in the dark building.

A tight humming excitement was in him. He walked around the room, running his hand over smooth panels, knurled knobs. He listened to his breathing and felt his pulse. His hands moved over the controls almost independently of thought. He set them for Beethoven, 1794. He stepped into the carpeted tapestried room where the Kempff recording of the first sonata still rested on the turntable. If he could live it just once more . . . His hands moved, attaching wires, taping electrodes, remembering. He lay on the couch for minutes. Then he got up, went back to the main room, returned all the switches to neutral, shut the lights off and went home.

Shortly after that he had an invitation from the Santessons. A cocktail party at their home in the West Eighties. He guessed it would be wearisome, but the night of the party he dressed anyway and took a cab crosstown. He had to go. In the past few years he had obligated himself. To tell the truth, Largens relied on these social functions to advance him where his talents alone might not. Seeing the uncompleted essay in his voicetyper, thinking of the rumors of personnel cutbacks, he knew he had to go. Any gesture of support from Santesson was welcome.

The apartment was elegant. The room was lit in soft blue. All the elder members of the Center were there, the aged coterie he had never before met informally. The elite. They had been born in the middle of the last century; some had studied with Stockhausen, Berio, Xenakis. The last legendary names of music.

Lia Santesson greeted him with a quick surprising press of her lips to his. Behind her was George Santesson, smiling warmly.

"Good of you to come, Charles."

He had the giddy, paranoiac feeling that they were all here for him, for his imminent prominence. The feeling increased as Lia led him through a gauntlet of introductions, her small electronic earrings making windchime noises as they walked, the old men's voices barely rising above the background of the party. They treated him with courtesy. He moved tentatively past their nods and smiles, a man exploring unsure ground.

The party's tempo was *adagio*. The guests all spoke softly, like low whispering strings; they moved like ancient clockwork. After a while Largens moved to a remote corner of the room. There was fatigue from the closed world of the party, which, somewhere, he realized was the same closed world as his life. *Adagio molto e cantabile.*

"Is that *you*, Charlie?"

The wonder in the voice stopped him. He turned. "I'm sorry?"

"David Kanigher, remember? The New Music Ensemble, what, fifteen years ago?"

"David! Of course!" Kanigher now wore glasses and an ineffective mustache, but was otherwise unchanged.

"Charlie. What have you been doing?"

And time shifted for Largens then: it stuttered and stopped and he was no longer at the Santessons' party, but somewhere liquid in his own mind, where the events of his life swept past him like a wave pulling sand from under his bare feet. He was there only with Kanigher, wondering how he could possibly explain his life's turnings to this stranger from the past. He felt a sudden cold twist of remorse. It might have been the liquor or the plummet of memory, but all at once it sickened him to be standing there, just past thirty-five years old, talking with a man whose ambitions he had once shared.

Young Largens had been the Center's *enfant terrible* in the days before he switched over to musicology. One of the few real talents. Then a criticism from Santesson had unmanned him. Though Santesson had been only forty then, he carried unmistakable authority, and what he said had struck Largens to the core: You've no heritage. No sense of the past in your music. Modern, superficial, shallow. Clever, but ultimately disappointing.

Of course it was what Largens had always feared about himself. He had been orphaned at thirteen, already an excellent pianist; he had been sent to relatives, an ancient aunt and uncle who had no piano and refused to let him waste time on music. It took him a full year to muster the courage to sue them and win the right to live in a state Montessori home. He grew up there with a hundred other youngsters, all bright and creative: artists, actors, poets. From then on, everyone in his life had been adept, but, he realized with adolescent smugness, none brilliant. That was for him. He was sure he had that spark of true greatness. And he feared that, like his playmates, he was really a talented dilettante.

So Santesson's comment had struck him to the core: *You've no heritage.* No parents, true. *No sense of the past.* But the past was those two shriveled tyrants, the past was cracked porcelain, the smell of urine and rose water. *Even Beethoven,* yes, the god, *that great innovator, had deep respect for his forerunners.* And Largens determined then to study music, to learn the history of music so well that no one could criticize him on that score, ever. Later he found it was a lifetime job.

"I'm in Beethoven Studies now," he said, the inside of his mouth like chalk.

"Are you composing?"

The cruel question. "No." Glancing around, he saw Lia Santesson watching him from fifty feet away. She smiled as their eyes met. He turned away.

"That's too bad, Charlie. You had the makings of a fine composer."

"Perhaps I did." Yes. The makings. Kanigher had learned the difference.

Kanigher smiled. "Did you know I was jealous of you?"

"Yes, I knew that." Certainly. The Ensemble playing an evening of new music: works by Stockhausen, Cage, Riley, Shapiro, and Largens. Kanigher found it so hard to work, while for Largens the music simply flowed from his pen. For that reason he had switched to musicology, believing he would always have that easy facility.

"What are *you* doing?"

"Scrambling for money. Would you believe it—I had to sell my piano last month! I've been using those dreadful Baldwin uprights in the Center basement. I have to spend an hour tuning before I can play, it's so damp down there."

"I don't understand. What about your salary?"

Kanigher spread his hands. "No more. All the money is going into your research equipment. They can't afford to keep unproductive composers on the payroll."

Largens' remorse found a small, hard comfort in that. "Unproductive?"

"Well, yes. I suppose I've become rather avant-garde, and I don't have the carapace for it. I'm too sensitive to criticism. And my, have they been criticizing. So I'm suffering through a block." Kanigher finished his drink. "They offered me a job teaching music history, which I turned down, and suddenly I was without a salary. My contract had a rather clever termination clause that I never read. It states that if I turn down any Center job when my own position is in jeopardy, I void the contract."

"So what's wrong with teaching history."

"Well, there's an awful lot of it going on." Kanigher paused. " 'If we carry our respect for the past too far, we are in danger of detaching ourselves from the present.' Andre Hodeir said that, a twentieth-century musicologist." He laughed. "You can tell I'm idle: I've been reading. But Christ, Charlie, I believe that. I'm terrified of losing the present. That's what music is all about, damn it! More than anything else, it's . . . a sense of what is necessary.

"You remember how clutched up I was with the Ensemble. Couldn't write anything. I had a girl then. She was so much better than anything I'd ever hoped for, it made everything a little unreal. I was sure I'd lose her, and I guess it was that sureness that finally drove her away. All right, I was just a young idiot. But Christ, when I lost her, I wrote music like I was born for it! Looking back, I can see that all I was doing was trying to hold those moments I had lost." Kanigher was quiet, and then he smiled. "I read through some of it the other day. It was a little embarrassing.

"But—now I feel I'm in danger of losing my composing. It makes me edgy and alert to little things, but totally useless in things that count. I'm afraid that's more serious than losing the girl, because then I knew I was young, I knew I could get over it, I knew I had my music and my friends. I'm a little older now, my only friends are acquaintances in the Center, and the music's all I have. It's too precious. I'm afraid to gamble it. I'm all too willing to take one of their jobs just to keep my muse safe and living in the style to which it's accustomed."

Largens looked at his drink. He shut his eyes. He looked up. "I wasn't afraid."

Kanigher stared at him a long time.

"I'm sorry, Charlie. Christ, I'm sorry. I thought you were happy."

"I'm all right."

"Santesson's been after me to study Beethoven."

"Why should he care what you do?"

"He seems to need these little conquests, displays of power. I'm sorry you're not happy, Charlie."

Santesson came over then. Liquor moved in Largens. He felt dead drained and set upon. Santesson smiled, a slow revelation of lion's teeth, and yet—with all his instincts burning in clear flame, Largens thought, *Why, he's afraid of Kanigher.* Why should a man intimate with Beethoven know such fear? And oddly, he had his answer: because Kanigher threatens him, Beethoven does not. Because Beethoven is dead. His music is fixed, pinned to the staves. Creation is a kind of magic that lives in men, and when they die it passes from them. Only the works remain. Santesson fears the potential: the actual he can master, with notes and diagrams and rules. In that second, Largens knew Santesson's power, and consequently his weakness. He felt some small magic stir in himself with that perception.

But Kanigher did not sense control of the situation resting on him. He retreated.

"Hello, David," Santesson said. "How's the composing coming?"

"Not very well, I'm afraid."

"Well, you know there's a place for you upstairs."

"Yes. I know. I'm considering it."

And as if that were all Santesson wanted he said, "Come, Charles, I have someone you should meet," and turned from Kanigher.

But Largens was aggressive. He had his first real motivation in much time. Suddenly, strangely, there was music in him. He wanted to get home and write it down. "I don't think I'll stay," he said.

Santesson stopped and studied him. "Do what you like, of course. I thought you'd like to meet your competition for the Beethoven job."

And Largens' breath left him. He followed Santesson and met a man named John Hart, a man with a feral look, and they spoke for a short time, saying nothing about the Beethoven job. It occurred to him that Santesson might have lied.

He finally broke free and made for the door, but was deftly caught by Lia Santesson. She chided him for ignoring her all evening, and started speaking in a low, oiled, intimate voice that eventually drew him out of his resolution and into an empty room with her. Into a warm, silken purgatory.

The last cry of a man dying, mad and forgotten, in the midst of a summer storm. Layers and levels and years away, the lightning flickered and the thunder rolled out of the hills over Largens as he died; then he opened his eyes and thought no: that's not me.

He raised himself on one elbow and looked panic-stricken into darkness. Then a faint numeric glow brought him back. It was just past 2 A.M. and he had been lying half under Lia Santesson's naked body for almost an hour, dozing. She was still asleep. He felt bad—seduced and soured with irresolution. Furtively he bent to whisper her awake, when he heard a gentle breathing behind him. A thin slice of light cut across the floor, over the bed and his calf. He pivoted at the waist and saw the large dark silhouette of George Santesson in the doorway. Light and the late remnants of the party were faintly behind him. Largens' mouth half opened, and he froze in that twisted stiff posture, in an agony of silence, in a waiting and a wanting to cry out, to explain, to accept punishment for his adultery if punishment were needed. He was riven by the thought of having hurt someone unaware. And then he was hotly ashamed, for *he* had been seduced, *he* had been led to this, as much by Santesson as by his wife. The big man did not move or speak. They stared at each other for almost a minute; then Santesson let out a slightly heavier breath and passed into the hall.

When Largens finally left, silent and exhausted and with no good-byes, the walk home woke him. It was much too late to go to sleep anyway, so he sat up with a single light on, reading through his old notebooks. He started to play a couple of his compositions, but they were demanding and his fingers were stiff, and the sound of the piano in the silent apartment was loud and plangent. It sounded much more assertive than he felt. He had to admit he had put it off too long.

He saw Santesson once more before the thing happened. Late one evening they passed in the hall and Largens was immediately and pointlessly embarrassed enough to rush for the elevators. Santesson stopped him and drew him gently aside and said, "I wanted to thank you for giving my wife what I can't."

The blood pounding through his temples turned cold. "Oh," he said; then: "Oh! I—" Then he said nothing, but gripped Santesson's arms and was gripped back. He felt he had been used, manipulated into it, yes—but he felt Santesson's sincerity too, the man's great deep pain and weakness. He pitied him.

"It's terribly hard sometimes," Santesson said, "to have to live here, now, when your soul is somewhere else; when the only thing that ever felt like home . . . is something you can't even touch. I've given so much to my music, to Beethoven." He seemed to struggle briefly. "You know the opening of the Ninth's third movement . . . the melodic theme?" Largens nodded. Santesson's mouth moved: "Mine."

"What?"

"I wonder what these transfers are, sometimes. What they've done to us. To the past. I sometimes think it's all one, there is no past or future, only that great timeless flow between. . . . I've had so many transfers; I've left so much of myself back there, Charles. I feel I've left my soul there." He shook his head. "Do you know what I mean?"

Largens could only nod.

"I'll let you go." He dropped his arms. "I have to do something. You're a good man, Charles."

The next morning Largens was interrupted from work by the sounds of a hallway commotion, from the direction of the transfer rooms. He walked into the hall; a cold intuition gripped him; he started to run. The door was open; people clustered. He forced his way through and found Grueder and a dozen others surrounding the red velvet couch. As he entered the tiny room, a doctor straightened, stethoscope limp in his hand. Grueder looked at Largens and said, "It's Santesson. He's dead."

The doctor said, "At your earliest convenience, Mr. Grueder," and went stiffly out. The others followed, murmuring.

Largens stared in incomprehension.

Grueder's face was strictured, a hard and ancient landscape strained by simply being. He sighed. "An unauthorized transfer. Santesson set up the equipment late last night after everyone left. He gave himself triple the required trigger voltage. It killed him."

"How?"

"His brain just shut off. His mind was no longer here and it couldn't come back."

Largens trembled. Santesson's body was still, composed. His face was peaceful. "The controls . . . where—?"

Grueder just shook his head. "It doesn't matter, Charles, he's dead. Wherever—whenever—he is, he's dead. Come—"

"Where?"

Grueder looked at him strangely.

"Beethoven. 1823."

Largens reeled. "The Ninth . . ."

"Yes. The Ninth." Grueder looked around, to make sure they were alone. "This was no accident, Charles. There was a note on his desk—I haven't told anyone this—he requested that you be appointed head of

209

Beethoven Studies. I think we can arrange to honor that wish. . . ."

"My God," Largens whispered, hardly hearing. He stared at the dead man's face, a poor snapshot exposure of a soul, a brief final connection of body and spirit. His heart, his brain, his body, were off, cold, stone; there was no way for Santesson to be alive. But Largens believed, he knew with fanatic irrationality, that some infinitesimal part of Santesson was living, almost two centuries in the past. . . .

"Did you hear, Charles? You're head of Beethoven Studies now."

"I heard."

"Don't mention this to anyone, Charles. Lord, if the government found out this was unauthorized, they'd shut us down in a second. The doctor suspects, but he can't prove anything, I hope. They only need a small excuse to end the program, so for God's sake keep quiet about it, Charles!" Largens sensed a threat behind that. He just nodded.

Something in Largens' silence sparked to Grueder. The old man looked at Santesson and sighed. "He had a hard life, Charles."

"So have we all."

4

For some time I have been occupied with major works. Much of the music has already hatched, at least in my head. I must first get them off my neck; two important symphonies, each one different from my others . . .

—Ludwig Van Beethoven, after completion of his Eighth Symphony.

The passage was circled in Santesson's notebook. The word *two* was underlined.

210

Largens walked out of the office with a confidence grown from a year of authority. "What is this stuff about a Tenth Symphony?"

Hart was there, serving as his assistant. He pushed the notebook back across the desk and snorted. "Nonsense. Santesson's pet theory. Some fragments of an unfinished symphony were found . . ."

"Yes, I *know* that, but a musicologist of Santesson's stature wouldn't make all these notes simply on that basis."

"Well, there they are."

A fine antagonism had been honed between the men. True to his word, Grueder had given Largens the appointment. Hart was still resenting it. And he had learned that to cut Largens he had only to insult Santesson. He added, "Personally I think the old boy went a bit *soft* toward the end." Stressing the *double entendre.*

For an instant Largens wanted to whirl the little man around, slap him across the face, shut him up. But the feeling passed, and he simply sighed, and walked out, allowing Hart his small victory.

He was thirty-six. It was winter. He was bitterly unhappy. Was that all the years were good for, to add an extra sting to the remorse?

Santesson's death had affected him deeply. The poor impotent bastard—escaping not even into death, but into a life not his own. Largens had had a brief affair with Lia; three months ago he had talked Kanigher into taking a musicology job; he did not know how much further he might fill Santesson's role.

He watched the setting sun bleed New York. The day turned red, was drawn off into Jersey. Central Park stretched below, the lights just coming on, a few couples strolling. The city was livable for the first time in a century: two million people now. Buildings were coming down crosstown. But it seemed so empty to him. He had grown up here when it was five times as dense.

Hart left without saying good-night. Largens heard the elevator chime, close, suck away. He felt very alone. He stepped into the hall, looking up and down. Lights off, doors sealed for the night. He walked down the corridor, passing no one, hearing nothing. He walked faster.

A strange feeling took hold of him.

By the time he reached the transfer room he was running.

He fumbled with his key, pressed it home; the door opened. He went in, sealed it, snapped on the lights.

The machinery waited.

(In case you ever need to. The whisper, razoring back to him, from a year away.)

(Santesson's escape.)

Quickly then, the patch. It was not as if he were breaking regulations: he had permission for this transfer; what matter when he took it? He was going back to the Ninth, he was going to consummate that lifelong obsession. His fingers twitched. His brain raced. At the last slider, marked *trigger voltage,* his fingers paused.

(Escape.)

1.5 he needed.

He slid it to 5.

A red light blinked, blinked, blinked.

(Escape!)

His hand trembled.

He brought it back to 1.5.

He had to rest for several minutes on the couch and let the sweat dry before he could take the drug. He taped electrodes to his skin, cold square steel invasions of his nakedness. He trembled there waiting for the colors to start, knowing he was wrong, knowing why he

212

couldn't tamper with the past this way, but he was too far gone in his need, the colors were on him, he reached for the trigger switch and *like that:* immediately went to sleep

and the center went away and left him spinning in a silver void, down and across cold currents of time that moved with the vast slowness of glaciers. He moved in directions he could not name. His metabolism was high with nerves and it panicked him to think what difference that might make and all the colors and the great rumbling shapes moved about him and he was afraid, God what've I done, he was climbing a wall of paranoia until he dropped off the top straight into sleep

and he shrugged it off with heavy blankets and a fear of suffocation. Bright morning sunlight was in the room. Intimations of the coming winter whispered across the sill. Beethoven stretched, rolled his legs out of bed. He quickly crossed the room, pulled on some woolen socks, and plunged his arms into a basin of icy water. Largens' consciousness seemed to splash into bright fragments at the shock and reform quivering, clearer, sharper. Beethoven started bellowing up and down scales. He toweled himself, went to the window overlooking Baden and sang a few measures from the symphony's second movement. He sang some more, paused, and made a pencil notation on the shutter, alongside a dozen others and lists of figures, sums, conversions from florins to guilders.

Then another researcher blinked into being. Santesson. Vibrations of interest, perhaps irony, reached him. Of course. This was a younger Santesson. And he suddenly realized, that was why Santesson had been so friendly and encouraging the first time. Santesson *knew* Largens would end up here sometime later. A fragment of Largens' future had been part of Santesson's memory.

Meanwhile, Beethoven's whole train of thought went past unnoticed. Largens let it. To hell with analysis: he was here for magic. He didn't care why Beethoven was writing the symphony, only that he was a part of it.

He wanted to be more a part of it.

So when Beethoven sat at the pianoforte to start work, Largens in effect *dictated* a phrase to him.

To his utter and terrified amazement, the composer stopped. His pen wavered in midstroke; it trembled with just a hint of suspicion as Largens' phrase roiled in his mind; then he jotted it down.

Crosstalk.

Beethoven had heard.

Some chemistry, some arcane connection of blood pressures, brainwaves, *something* had bridged the gap—and now Beethoven was developing a passage from his theme. *What had he done?*

This was not the Ninth Symphony; and yet the music spattered out from the pen, not entirely his, not all Beethoven's. His panic increased. What were the mechanics of music, time, the past?

Music was articulated time. Largens always thought of it as a river. If he were lucky, relaxed and easy in his craft, a man could tap the flow, turn the currents of time to something solid, a piece of music. And rarely, so rarely, he might actually direct the flow. Time might swirl and bend around him as space bends around a point of gravity. Beethoven had that force; that was his magic. But Beethoven was unique. What of himself and the critics that with machineries, with tinkerings and tamperings dammed the flow? What were they doing to the past?

The next few hours were blurred and broken. Largens had no sense of returning to 2016. He remem-

214

bered Santesson's voice, among all the other phantom voices filling Beethoven's head. The opening of the third movement—but not the way Largens remembered it. He lost all track of time then and came finally to consciousness in the dark transfer room, drained and sick with the irresponsibility of what he had done. He skirted Central Park on the way home, feeling vaguely threatened by it, watching the night sky glow faintly through layers of leaves that shifted as he walked under them. The way the layers crossed and moved stirred something in him. It reminded him of the surrealistic moments of transfer. It gave him unpleasant intimations, as if the trees were trying to tell him something; or, more accurately, his mind was searching for a way to reach him, and the trees were handy. *Something is different.* He was too tired to think about it. He stopped in a bar on Sixty-eighth Street, had three drinks and went home. He had trouble with his door key—he had to search his ring for it, which seemed far too crowded—got inside, and dropped onto the bed.

The benefit of living in a closed world was that you were effectively shielded from attack from without. The failing was that your defenses weakened, and if the closed world started to come apart, you were helpless.

Charles Largens' world had showed the first weak seam. He lay drunk in his bed and cried as he hadn't since his parents died.

The afternoon before the official transfer he spent with Lia. In the same apartment on East Eighty-fourth, they traded thoughts and intimacies. He spoke as in a dream:

"Does it seem different to you?"

"What?"

"The way things are."

"What things?"

"Everything; I don't know. You and I and

The apartment on Seventy-eighth Street was unchanged since Santesson's death; Lia lived alone there and he visited frequently. This morning

He was so confused now, the world seemed only a welter of possibilities, nothing was certain. The sense of *change* that followed each of his returns had disjointed him so

A thin drizzle grayly painted the bedroom window as they

No, no; it was not real, it couldn't be. He was dreaming, the dreams timeless monuments of time, clear and precise, their meanings faint and distant. These dreams had no more reality, no less importance, than all the music he had never written.

His dreams now, his nightdreams, were of Beethoven and the past, of music unraveling itself into spaghetti piles, and he woke frequently in sweat and fear, lying still but sliding madly into the past: time and the tide took him back, the great bulk of days he had lived weighed more heavily than days he would yet live, freighted him toward the past. It was only necessary to stand still in that awful darkness to be drawn vertiginously back.

And one morning, *that* morning he walked to the Center in a surreal mood, living in a fantasy of the near-future which was a baroque counterpointed dream of the past since he was dreaming of where he would be in a half hour which would be two hundred years in the past, and concurrently he was remembering all the times in his past he had daydreamed of this moment, each disparate present a window on the past through the future, and how different it all was from how he had frequently thought it would be. He had now a fear of alternate presents, vague suspicions of what was happening to him, to time, to music. He thought of how hectic his time with Beethoven would be with all the researchers from past and future history converging on that most covetable moment of inspiration.

(He had spent one afternoon with Bach during the Brandenburg months, during his assistantship to Santesson, and had been so drained by the babel of thoughts from the dozen others also there that he quite forgot why he had come. His own thoughts were washed from him in the greater cataract; there was only the sound of all the critics that would ever inhabit Bach during that period—a dozen trains converging on the same terminus from different moments in time, with a tumult and a clattering and collision, Bach, the terminus, all ignorant of the chaos within.)

(Or had all that furious racket somehow fueled the headlong counterpoint of the Brandenburg concerti? No, ridiculous, stop it.)

But he walked into the transfer room now with a growing apocalyptic sense, his every instinct so tightly wound that they had to give him a tranquilizer with the drug; and at the moment of triggering he still screamed, screamed his way into *the place without time, the place* of motion without destination, form without function, research without purpose, the floating fragments of times without order. Time without his world, times without Beethoven, times where his own life was rich and glorious; and in an instant quickly past he heard his song cycle finished, he heard half a score symphonies that were his own; he clutched at them and they vanished, and only the flat spinning emptiness remained, as distant and unreachable as the bowl of the sky. . . . The moire patterns slowed, the layers peeled back to show greater complexities, more permutations, fork upon fork of time, and then a great rending—

(there was a time as a boy he had lain by midnight railroad tracks, waiting for a train to pass, the air hot, muggy, iron-smelling; he waited till a glow appeared, distant, and grew to a full glare; and then the train was upon him and rushing past like doom and time and the endless vacuum of space wrapped in a midnight earth blackness, the air shuddering and sucking all around him, the very fabric of space torn with its force. He felt his heart clutch up, stall, and he felt the end of the world passing in that endless second. Time suspended. He felt that now, in the moment of transfer, in the region between times.)

—as blocks of time were torn by their roots, knocked free and avalanched

: all past in an instant.

1823. Baden.

He was there; and the first thing was *not* a clear idyllic vision of the past, but a riot-blur of graygreen light and the assault of a thousand nightmare conversations of which he heard no words—

but Beethoven was *deaf*—

but the voices of a thousand and more men from Largens' time filled the void with their own sounds and laments, voices of pain and frustration and everything Largens saw coming to fruition in himself, voices of humanity enough to crush him—

then strangely they all fell silent—

a tense waiting hush, as before a curtainrise—

. . . and Beethoven thought clearly of the fourth

movement of his Ninth Symphony, musing, brooding, on the proper introduction to Schiller's Ode . . .

and the voices surged out of silence:

O Freunde, nicht diese Töne! Sondern lasst uns ausgenehmere anstimmen und freudevollere . . .

Beethoven staggered and gasped. He tore open his notebook.

The voices—!

Beethoven's tortured mind sensed them, it caught all the thunder and roar of a thousand voices, all gabbling humanity; they struck off his mind like a scream off piano strings, fragmenting into tones and harmonies:

Freude, schöner Gotterfunken, Tochter aus Elysium . . .

He scribbled frantically, desperately, and they urged him on, the minds pressed and sang and screamed, pleaded with him to say for them the things they couldn't, and Beethoven was filled with pity, understanding, a community of despair . . .

Seid umschlungen, Millionen, dieser Kuss der ganzen Welt . . .

and harder they pressed, each with his own personal demands and pains, each in search of his own special magic, a thousand variations of the Ninth, a thousand personal misinterpretations spilling their own lost songs into the chaos—

Deine Zauber binden wieder, was die Mode streng getheilt . . .

Largens caught the roar of an electronicized version, metal resonances echoing through Beethoven's deaf mind, a confusion of sounds, reverberating, building, starting to topple this immense structure, and in the chaos he recognized Santesson's voice, and then his own, all singing with the mad intensity they had never trusted their own lives to reach, a tottering sea of

219

sound, climbing and accelerating, oh they knew what was coming, they *knew* it! madly racing, *screaming—*

Ja, wer auch nur eine Seele, sein nennt auf dem Erdenrund!

Und wer's nie gekonnt der stehle, weinend sich aus diesem Bund ...

until it was too much, too much pressure, and there was a rending and a piercing cry of anguish that was Beethoven's own as he *saw* what was inside him, and the turmoil raged on and on, past the end of the music—

(the last cry of a man dying, mad and forgotten, in the midst of a summer storm. The lightning flickered and the thunder rolled out of the hills over Largens as he died; then he opened his eyes and thought, Oh my God, it's me, it is, it's me and Santesson and all the rest, all the failed and weak and impotent ... but it's not Beethoven.)

Silence ...

Somewhere outside it was raining, fat drops hammering and spraying his face, and unheard thunder shaking the earth ...

and inside the chaos raged on and rose over Largens as all the occupants wept and muttered about their own misspent lives (and the composer was silent, silent) and they at least rested in this dark world of gray ash, this mind burnt and made their own—

(and Largens strained to hear Beethoven, but there was silence, silence, only silence—)

until the recall, and with great relief he heard the raining silence fall away, recede like foaming surf into sand, and he heard:

"You okay?"

The lights were soft and warm: inside lights. The sky's cold gray was gone. He was back.

"Uh." Speech was an effort. "Yeah. Are—are you the one who strapped me in?"

"Yeah. You're all right, you're sure?"

"Uh huh." Largens' voice was quite flat. "You look different."

The attendant smiled. "They all say that after they've been through the breakdown."

"Breakdown?"

"Yeah. The 1823 breakdown you went to study, remember?" The attendant shook his head with old amusement. "Every time, you guys forget."

"I . . . I went to study the Ninth . . ."

"The what?"

"The Ninth, the Ninth Symphony! The Chorale on Schiller's 'Ode to Joy!' "

"Hey, take it easy. Beethoven only wrote *eight* symphonies, remember? There were fragments for the Ninth, but no more."

"No!" Largens sat up suddenly, and the room tilted. In his vertigo he felt thoughts rushing away and he tried to hold them.

"Poor guy," the attendant said, peeling tape from wires. "First he loses his hearing, then his sanity. Never wrote another note."

Largens was sick, soul-sick. The room spun without spinning.

They had killed the Ninth Symphony. All the frustrated pianists and composers and singers turned scholars had brought their frustration to the works they studied; and they had brought it to Beethoven himself. All their souls' cheapnesses summed; the faint crosstalk turned to a shout. They had brought their weakness and despair in such pent-up furious quantity that Beethoven had been swamped by it, and drowned.

Largens saw layers of reality peeling away, shifting, each one new with each new transfer, each time an-

221

other subtle alteration: past present future so closely bound and interwoven there was no way *not* to change them.

This time they had killed the Ninth. This time Beethoven had gone mad in 1823. But next time—after the next transfer, what might happen? Would there be seven symphonies, or six, or four? As the thousands converged earlier and earlier in the master's life in coming realities, in search of unworked time, when would the breakdown occur? After a few more years of indiscriminate transfers, would the young Beethoven ever leave Bonn to study with Haydn? Or would he rebel against his tyrannical father and never touch the piano after the old man's death?

It was all so delicately balanced.

And he felt the reality of the Ninth leaving him, a great weight lifting; his memories slid and shifted and there was a great surge of loss. How, how did it go?

Freude ...

He tried to hear, to remember, but there was only the silence, deafening and mute.

A terrible long night. Sleepless, he listened to faraway traffic and watched snow hit his window. He had dreams while he was awake. Dreams in which the building moved. In which the room filled with water, then emptied of air. The window vanished and he was left in complete blackness. He got up and walked around in the blackness. He walked at least a quarter of a mile straight into it. Then he was in bed again. He went to visit his aunt and uncle. They yelled at him. He forced open his uncle's dresser with a claw hammer and got out the pistol he kept there and shot both of them. There was a large grand piano in the living room when he tried to leave. He couldn't get past it. Later he was in a cemetery, knocking over stones. The ground was very dry and loose and they went over easily. When he saw the old composer walk stiffly around the room, lecturing, he went to sleep.

He woke at two in the afternoon and took a cold shower. Without thinking, he called the government agency. He then dressed and dictated two letters to his voicetyper. He mailed one and took the other with him. He walked directly to Grueder's office. The old man was hanging up the phone when he entered.

"Charles." He looked pale and shaken. "Something awful has happened. The government's found out about our unauthorized transfers."

Largens slid his envelope across the table. Grueder only glanced at it.

"They're sending investigators. They're sure to close us down."

"So?"

"So? No more transfers!"

"I called them."

Grueder looked at him dumbly. "You. I didn't trust you at first. Then I did."

"I had a little talk with Beethoven last night. Or with myself, or with whatever remnants of Beethoven are in me. He said it might be too late, but I'd never know if I didn't try."

"This is incredible. You'll regret this, Largens!"

"I may."

"You idiot! What are you going to do now, compose?"

"I think so."

"You can't walk away from it that easily!"

"Yes I can," Largens said.

He went outside. He was shaking. If it had gone on, all Beethoven's music might have gone. What would the world—his world—be like without Beethoven?

Still, he was afraid he had made a terrible mistake.

The silence—a silence with specific dimensions, a silence in four movements—haunted him. Could he ever make up for that?

Despair rose in him as he stood there with no place to go. Then he remembered about inaction and time and the tide that wanted to draw him back. He took a step and then another and soon he was walking home, entering the second half of his life.

Why, I'm a young man, he thought. I'm two hundred years younger than I was yesterday. I can do something with that.

What was necessary was to begin.